The Ship that Flew

It was a tiny ship, not longer than six inches, carved in some old dark wood . . .
'Could I buy it, do you think?'
Then the old man said a strange thing.
'It would cost all the money you have in the world—and a bit over.'

When Peter sees the model ship in the shop window, he wants it more than anything else on Earth. But this is no ordinary model. The ship takes Peter and the other children on magical flights, wherever they ask to go. They fly around the world, and back into the past. They meet Robin Hood, an Egyptian Pharaoh, and the Norse gods in Asgard. Time after time the magic ship takes them on different exciting adventures. And why should magic ever end?

HILDA LEWIS was born in London, and lived for much of her life in Nottingham. She wrote many historical novels, mostly for adults. Of her children's novels, the classic story is *The Ship that Flew*, first published in 1939.

To MrS. Pinniger

from Glenn

Other Oxford Children's Modern Classics

The Eagle of the Ninth
Rosemary Sutcliff

Outcast
Rosemary Sutcliff

The Silver Branch
Rosemary Sutcliff

The Lantern Bearers
Rosemary Sutcliff

Minnow on the Say
Philippa Pearce

HILDA LEWIS

The
SHIP
That
FLEW

Oxford University Press
Oxford New York Toronto

Oxford University Press, Great Clarendon Street, Oxford OX2 6DP

Oxford New York
Athens Auckland Bangkok Bogota Bombay
Buenos Aires Calcutta Cape Town Dar es Salaam Delhi
Florence Hong Kong Istanbul Karachi
Kuala Lumpur Madras Madrid Melbourne
Mexico City Nairobi Paris Singapore
Taipei Tokyo Toronto Warsaw

and associated companies in
Berlin Ibadan

Oxford is a trade mark of Oxford University Press

A CIP catalogue record for this book is available
from the British Library

Cover illustration by Paul Hunt

ISBN 0 19 271768 5

Printed and bound in Great Britain
by Biddles Ltd, Guildford and King's Lynn

Foreword

In the summer of 1937, when the clouds of war were already gathering over Europe, I went with my parents on holiday to Normandy. I was then seven years old, and had taken nothing with me to read. My mother, Hilda Lewis, already an established novelist, had never written a book for children, and she started to write this story of a magic ship which carried a family of four children through time and space to whatever destination they chose.

The book eventually became *The Ship that Flew*, and was published by Oxford University Press in 1939. It was frequently reprinted, and it has been translated into several languages. It has however been out of print for some years.

I am very pleased that Oxford University Press have decided to republish this book some 55 years after it originally appeared. My grandchildren Eve and Edmund are now much the same age as I was when the book was written. I hope that it will give as much pleasure to them and to children of their age as it gave me all those years ago.

HUMPHREY LEWIS
1993

For

Humphrey

with my love

CONTENTS

Foreword   v
1. The Magic Begins   1
2. And Continues   11
3. The First Adventure   25
4. The Land of the Nile   38
5. Adventure in a Bazaar   48
6. Frey's Ship   66
7. Matilda   82
8. Matilda's Tower   100
9. The Valley of the Kings   114
10. To the Time of Usertsen   137
11. The Lion of Justice   150
12. Matilda Comes   164
13. Matilda Goes   185
14. The Specially Exciting Adventure   207
15. Dickon   221
16. The Flying-ship Goes Home   237

Note to the Reader

This book was written many years ago, and some things have changed since then—such as the money the characters use, and the way that they speak. But some things never change—things like the excitement of having your very own flying ship, and the wonder of the adventures that the children have here.

CHAPTER 1
The Magic Begins

It all began with Peter's toothache. You wouldn't think anything really nice could come out of having a toothache, would you? Well, this time it did. But I had better go right back to the beginning and explain.

There were four of them. Peter and Sheila and Humphrey and Sandy—which is short for Alexandra—Grant. Their father was a doctor at Radcliff. At least he didn't live in Radcliff itself, which is a popular little sea-side town, but just outside, in Radcliff Village, where the houses are old, and set back from the road in large gardens, shaded in summer by ancient trees. The people who live in these old houses turn up their noses at Radcliff, though I can't think why, because Radcliff is just as pretty in *its* way. It is a nice bright little town with lots of jolly shops, and you can get pink rock with Radcliff stamped right through it, and ice-cream cornets every yard or so. And if that isn't nice I should like to know what is!

The children who live in Radcliff Village aren't encouraged to go into Radcliff during the months of July and August which are called 'The season' and they are *never* allowed to go in by themselves; for one thing, the roads are dangerous then because of all the cars dashing up and down

1

the High Street, which is the only important street. There are other reasons, too, but that is the best one.

Did I say *never* allowed? Well that was a mistake, because Peter was allowed. Once. Because of his toothache.

When Peter had toothache his mother always took him in to see Mr. Frinton, and when Mr. Frinton had finished doing good work on Peter's teeth, mother always took him out to tea, and gave him a pink-and-white ice when it was in season and pink-and-white rock when it wasn't, because when your visit to the dentist is over you are allowed to eat anything—if you are careful.

Well, this particular day mother couldn't take him because she was ill. She was in a nursing-home in fact, but the children didn't know that, because mother and father didn't think children ought to be worried with grown-up things. So father called Peter into his study, which was also the room where he saw his patients, and said,

'Listen, old man,' and then Peter knew that father wanted him to do something really grown-up, because he always called him *old man* on those occasions. Then father explained that there wasn't any one to take Peter into Radcliff so Peter would have to go by himself.

'But you can manage perfectly well,' said father, 'because you're sensible and grown-up. Here's a shilling for your fare, and a shilling for your tea, and a shilling for yourself if Mr. Frinton says you've been brave. You must ask him before you keep that shilling. There's a bus at 2.10, and you'd better take a return; there'll be twopence change.'

So Peter went upstairs to the bathroom to wash his face,

and he was particularly careful to clean his teeth which is a thing you must never forget to do when you visit the dentist. There was an excited sort of feeling inside him, partly because of going into Radcliff by himself, and partly because of being brave about Mr. Frinton. There was sixpence in his money-box and he got it out with a knife and put it in his pocket, because it might come in useful just in case he didn't get that extra shilling.

Peter caught the bus and paid his fare. But whether it was that he didn't speak up, or whether the conductor wasn't listening, I don't know, but he only got a single ticket into Radcliff. Peter was a little bit sorry, because now he'd have to take that extra twopence off his shilling if he was brave, or off his tea-money or his sixpence if he wasn't, because father had distinctly mentioned a return-ticket. But as it happened, it all turned out for the best, as Peter had to admit when he thought about it afterwards.

Well, he went to Mr. Frinton's and he *was* brave, and Mr. Frinton said so without being asked; and as it was early Peter thought he would stroll about Radcliff and have a good look round.

He strolled about looking into the windows of all the bright little shops. They all seemed to be selling the same kind of thing, Peter thought—china with coats of arms on it, and buckets and spades, and paddling-shoes and bathing-suits and toys.

Peter looked at the toys but he couldn't see anything he wanted. There were kites, but he had a kite. And balls, but he had several balls. And jigsaws and cricket-bats. There were other things, too, but they cost much more than one and six.

The Ship That Flew

'What I'd really like,' Peter said to himself, 'is a boat, a nice little boat, but that would cost a good deal more than one and six.'

He looked carefully at all the cheap boats in all the windows, but they *looked* cheap; the paint was sticky and they weren't a good shape. 'They wouldn't balance,' Peter thought sadly. He decided that he would go down to the beach and have a look at the pierrots; then he would give himself a glass of milk and some shiny brown buns and a pink-and-white ice, and then catch the six o'clock bus home.

So he took the first turning that led down to the sea.

It was a narrow little street and rather dark, with old houses set close together. Peter was rather surprised. He didn't remember this street, and what was more, he hadn't known there were any old houses in new little Radcliff-on-sea. 'But then,' he told himself sensibly, 'I don't know *everything*!'

On the left-hand side of the dark little street was a dark little shop; such a dark little shop that you could hardly make out what it sold. Peter crossed the road and stared into the dark little window. He could just make out an old oak table covered with blue-and-white saucers and strings of beads and a couple of copper kettles.

And then all of a sudden his heart gave a great jump. Because he saw it. He saw it, and he fell in love with it immediately.

It was a tiny ship, not longer than six inches, carved in some old dark wood. He stared at it so long that, in spite of the dimness of the window, he could make out everything about the ship—the tiny round shields, smaller than threepenny bits, that hung over the sides, and the boar's head carved and gilt, that seemed to grin at Peter in a friendly manner, though it was a very fierce boar indeed.

Peter wondered how much the little boat would cost. It would cost a great deal he was certain, and yet he couldn't go away and leave the dear little boat, the friendly little boat behind. And then, suddenly, without knowing just how it happened, he was standing inside the dark little shop.

A tiny far-off bell tinkled and stopped. Nothing happened. Peter went on standing there afraid to move, in case he knocked something precious off a table with his elbow, or trod on something precious with his foot.

It seemed to him that he stood there a long time without any-thing happening. He was just thinking that he had better open the door and let himself out into the street, when something happened. He heard the sound of far-off steps coming from somewhere at the back of the house. They came nearer and nearer, and then an old man stood beside him. He was a very old man indeed, and over one eye he wore a black patch.

'What can I do for you?' asked the old man.

'Please,' said Peter, 'could you tell me the price of the little ship, the one in the window?'

The old man didn't stir. He just stood there looking hard at Peter.

'You like that little ship?' he asked at last.

Peter nodded. He couldn't explain just how much he *did* like it.

The old man moved towards the crowded little window.

'They don't make ships like that nowadays,' he said a little sadly.

'Is it very old?' Peter asked, hoping that it wasn't, because very old things, he knew, often cost a good deal of money.

The old man nodded. 'Older than any one would believe,' he said softly, stroking the tiny ship with gentle hands.

'She's a beauty!' Peter said with all his heart.

'Yes, she *is* a beauty!' agreed the old man, holding it as carefully as if it were an egg that he might drop.

'How much is it?' Peter asked, his heart beating very fast.

'All the money in the world wouldn't have bought this once,' the old man answered, 'no, not if it were prince nor king nor emperor himself.'

Peter didn't know what to say to this, so he said, 'Could I buy it, do you think?'

Then the old man said a strange thing. 'It would cost all the money you have in the world—and a bit over.'

Peter put his hand in his pocket and pulled out his money. There were two silver shillings, a sixpence, a threepenny-bit and three pennies neatly spread out on the dark counter.

'Three shillings is the price,' said the old man gravely and put the little boat into Peter's hands.

It was only when Peter stood outside blinking in the sunshine after the darkness of the shop, that he remembered that he had spent his tea money, which didn't matter much, and the twopence belonging to his father which mattered rather more, and his fare money which mattered a good deal.

Yes, he had done what the old man had said. Without realizing it, he had paid all he had in the world—and a bit over. Well, as for the twopence, he would borrow it from one of the others and pay it back next week, but if he meant to get home that night he had better start right away. And then he remembered the short cut across the sands.

He heard the big clock on the bandstand boom out one, two, three, four, five.

'If I hurry, I can do it easily,' he told himself.

He gave his little ship one last loving look and then put it carefully into his pocket. It was only when he was striding along the firm wet sand, his shoes dangling by their laces from his neck, that he remembered something and whistled.

The ship was at least six inches long—and he hadn't a pocket that size. And yet it had slipped quite easily into his pocket.

He took the ship out of his pocket and looked at it again. Yes, it was six inches. And over. Nearer eight, as far as he could judge. He put it back again. It slipped in easily. 'Must have been something the dentist put in my tooth that makes me muddled,' he thought and went on whistling.

He was as happy as a king. The bad tooth was out and his little ship was in his pocket. His fingers kept playing with it as he walked. He was wondering what the others would think of it. The girls wouldn't care for it much of course, but Humphrey would love it. He wondered whether Humphrey would clean out the rabbit-hutch if he were allowed to handle the new ship.

He wandered on, his mind full of his new toy. He had forgotten where he was. And what was more important, he had forgotten the time.

Now it was a great mistake to forget the time. The greatest

mistake of all. And I will tell you why. It was because Peter's way lay round a tiny bay which was the most dangerous for miles around. The beach sloped suddenly down from the cliffs to the sea, and when the tide came in, it came with a rush and a pour and a swirl to the cliff's edge. The water in this little bay would be deep and dangerous even when the tide was not full elsewhere.

And there was Peter strolling along that very bay, whistling, and his fingers playing inside his pocket where the boat lay.

Suddenly he raised his head. Then he stopped dead still, staring at the tangle of green and yellow water that was racing towards him.

He looked wildly about him. The cliffs rose sheer and white and unfriendly on all sides. Before him the oncoming waves swept inwards, drew back with a sucking noise over stone and pebble, swept inwards again, spreading their pattern of yellow lacy foam nearer and nearer.

Peter was frightened. More frightened than he had ever been in his life before. All sorts of ideas came muddling into his head. . . . His mother and father—his brother, and the sisters he would never see again.

He said a little prayer and felt rather braver. But not so very brave.

The water was so near now that it was licking over his bare toes. He gave a little groan. He said aloud, 'I wish, I *wish* I could get home!'

There was a tugging inside his pocket, as though something was moving, something like a bird, something that strained and strained to be free. Without knowing what he was doing, Peter put his hand in his pocket and drew out the ship.

It began to grow in his hand.

He stared at it in amazement. The water was up to his knees. But he had forgotten the water. The boat was growing larger and larger. It was floating gently on the waves. A bright sail unfurled itself.

The ship was just large enough to hold one little boy.

Peter scrambled over the edge. The sail spread itself. The golden boar was dazzling in the sunshine. The ship rose slowly into the air.

It held a steady course above the tumbling foaming sea, above the white cliff wall it rose, above the green cliff-tops where people walked and raised their eyes to the wonderful bird of gold and scarlet and blue.

On flew the boat. And on flew Peter, not knowing whether he was on his head or his heels.

Magic. Magic had happened to him. He knew it would some day. He had always believed in magic, even when the others had laughed at him, laughed because he was the eldest and ought to know better.

He leaned over and patted the side of the ship. He had to clutch hold tightly for he nearly fell out. He was not yet used to flying in a magic ship.

When he looked again, he saw that they were dropping, although the movement was so gentle he had not noticed it. Tree tops floated up to meet him and floated away again. Roofs of houses went by like red mushrooms. The green earth rose up to meet him. With the gentlest movement, like a butterfly settling, the keel of the boat touched the grass.

Peter stepped out. But this time he didn't stare, because magic had become the most natural thing in the world to him.

The bright sails were rolling themselves up. The boat was shrinking, shrinking, shrinking. Soon there was nothing to be seen but the toy that had so taken Peter's fancy. He picked it up gently from the grass, wrapped it in his handkerchief for fear of damaging it, and put it in his pocket. Then he looked round. He was on the cliff path that sloped downward to the house.

He was whistling like a thrush as he ran down the path to meet the others.

CHAPTER 2

And Continues

The others met him at the end of the cliff walk. They had been waiting for him, hanging over the garden gate. They had been taking it in turns to go to the corner where the bus stopped in order to see if he were coming. They wanted him to come back quickly because it was dull without him, for he always had such good ideas for new games. There was another reason, too. They were hoping he would bring back with him a piece of that pink rock he would most certainly buy. Of course they would be too polite to mention such a thing unless he did, but Sandy had a large stone in her pocket which she meant to offer when the moment came for breaking the rock. That is, of course, the best way of breaking rock; you should *never* try with a knife, it is much too dangerous.

'You *have* been a long time,' shouted Sheila as soon as she caught sight of him.

'Why didn't you come by bus?' shouted Humphrey even louder.

Sandy didn't shout anything. She thought it was the wrong moment for asking questions; it distracted one's attention from the pink rock that was probably reposing in Peter's pocket.

'Did it hurt?' asked Humphrey without waiting for an
answer to his first question.

'Did what hurt?' Peter asked, having forgotten so unim-
portant a thing as having a tooth out.

'The tooth!' Sandy explained impatiently with both eyes
on his pocket.

'Oh, that!' Peter's voice was airy. 'Oh, no! In fact I'd
forgotten all about it!'

Three pairs of eyes went as round as sixpences.

'I don't believe you went!' said Sheila at last.

Peter didn't answer. He opened his mouth and the
children inspected it one after another.

'Isn't he brave?' said Humphrey at last.

'Oh, I don't know!' remarked Peter remembering how far
from brave he had felt with the deep water racing towards
him. 'Not very,' he added truthfully.

'Let's look at it,' said Sandy, not because she really wanted
to see the tooth, but because she hoped that putting his hand
in his pocket might bring out something much more
interesting.

And so it did.

Outstretched on Peter's palm lay the tiny ship.

'Gosh!' said Humphrey and came closer to look.

'It's a darling!' said Sheila.

'Pooh!' said Sandy who was disappointed and didn't mind
showing it.

Peter wrapped the boat up again and slipped it back into
his pocket. 'Sit down!' he said in the commanding sort of
voice he had at times. Sometimes it annoyed the others and

they wouldn't obey, but now there was something about him
that made them want to listen. They sat down on the grass
and Peter sat down in front of them.

'Before I begin,' he said very solemnly, 'you've got to take
the oath.'

The three children looked up eagerly. The oath was only
used on very special occasions.

Peter held out his two hands, the middle finger of each
crossed tightly over the first one. The other three children
held out theirs, crossed in the same manner. Peter touched
them lightly with his own. Then the four of them chanted
slowly,

> *Earth and water and fire and air,*
> *We solemnly promise, we solemnly swear,*
> *Not a word nor a look nor a sound to declare,*
> *Earth and water and fire and air!*

It all sounded very grand chanted like that in the open air,
though Sandy wasn't at all sure about the meaning of the earth-
and-water-and-fire part. Sheila, who had composed it, said
rather crossly when the point was raised, that it didn't matter a
bit because it sounded lovely and it rhymed and the two middle
lines were plain as a pikestaff so what did it matter?

And when you come to think about it, she was right.

Peter said, 'Listen. When Mr. Frinton was finished with
me, I thought I'd walk down to the front. I wanted to see the
pierrots. Well, I cut across the High Street and I took a
turning—all of them lead down to the sea of course—and I
found myself in a little old street—'

'There aren't any old streets in Radcliff,' Sheila reminded
him, 'they're all as new as new!'

'A little old street,' Peter went on as though he hadn't heard, and then spoilt the effect by adding, 'I was there and you weren't!'

'But you couldn't have been.' It was Humphrey interrupting this time, 'because Sheila's right. There isn't a single old street in Radcliff, not one. I know them all by heart because of my map; it shows every street in Radcliff.'

Sandy said, 'If Huff says so, he's right. He's a walking atlas.'

'If you all know better than me,' Peter said nastily, 'you can tell the tale yourselves.' And he stood up to go. Sheila scrambled to her feet and went after him quickly. 'Sorry Pete,' she said. 'Go on! We're dying to hear. You *know* we are!'

She put her arm through his and turned him round to face the others.

'I expect you're right,' Humphrey said humbly, 'I expect they forgot to put your street in the map because it's so old.'

'Oh, do go on!' exclaimed Sandy who didn't believe in apologizing too much.

Peter sat down on the grass and went on with his story.

'I didn't come home by bus,' he said slowly.

'We know that,' Sandy interrupted, 'because—'

Sheila and Humphrey glared at her and she subsided.

'You must have been awfully quick coming home by the cliffs,' Sheila said admiringly, 'it's ever such a long way round.'

Peter said impatiently, 'I didn't come along the cliffs, either. I came across the sand.'

14

Nobody said a word. Peter knew what they were all thinking. He said, 'I don't expect you to believe me. I know it's been high tide for ages. I can't really believe it myself even though it happened.'

'What happened?' the three children asked together.

'Look!' Peter said, and once more he drew the tiny boat from his pocket and set it on the grass.

There it lay, its fierce boar's head grinning, its bright little sail tightly rolled, and its tiny shields flashing in the sunshine.

They went on looking. The tiny ship lay peacefully on the bright grass.

'Well?' Sheila said at last. 'When does the story begin?'

Peter was staring at it. There was a puzzled expression on his face. Why, oh why, didn't it show them its magic power? Why didn't it grow?

'I came back in that,' he said at last.

Humphrey and Sandy burst out laughing, but Sheila, who was older, could see that Peter was in deadly earnest. She sent them a fierce look and the laughter was cut short. She went quickly over to Peter and touched him on the arm.

'It's that stuff the dentist uses,' she said kindly, 'it does that to me, too!'

Peter shook her off angrily.

'It's true, I tell you, *true*! I was coming round by the point. I was nearly drowned. But the ship brought me home. It flew. Like a bird, I tell you.'

'Yes,' Sheila said soothingly, 'don't you think we ought to go in now? It's awfully hot in the sun!'

Peter looked very angry indeed. Then he took a deep breath. They could see he was trying to control himself.

'You don't believe me,' he said at last. 'Well I don't expect you to! I wouldn't myself unless I saw it with my own eyes. But I wish, I *wish* it would happen. I wish the ship would take us somewhere—anywhere!'

Still the little ship lay on its side, its tiny shields winking in the sunshine.

'Where would you go if you could choose?' asked Sandy, not because she wanted to know, but for the sake of filling in an awkward pause.

'I don't care. Anywhere. Just to show you. Back to Radcliff, even!'

He turned his back so that they shouldn't see his lips quivering. He was beginning to agree with Sheila that it might have been the dentist's stuff. So the magic hadn't happened at all! Everything was perfectly ordinary in a perfectly ordinary world!

He stared unhappily out over the blue and silver sea.

Suddenly Humphrey gave a cry of pure astonishment. Sandy rolled over to stare at him. Sheila did nothing, for she was already staring as though her eyes were about to pop out of her head.

'Look!' cried Humphrey again, and his voice was breathless with wonder.

Peter turned slowly on his heel.

It was happening.

The little boat was growing, steadily and surely growing. It was a foot long. A yard long. It was large enough to hold one child, and Peter stepped on board. It was large enough to hold two, and Sheila followed him. It went on growing, and

Humphrey clambered in. It grew still larger, and Sandy, looking as if she couldn't believe it and was still in the middle of a dream, followed them.

The ship stopped growing.

Sheila murmured faintly, 'It's the sun. We ought to have worn hats.'

Humphrey said in a funny little voice, 'It's a dream. I'm dreaming it. You've all come into my dream!'

'*My* dream!' said Sandy in the kind of voice that means to go on arguing.

'It isn't a dream,' Peter said happily. 'It's happening. And it's real.'

The boat began to rise steadily in the air with a strong and even motion. Peter said, 'I wonder why it didn't happen when I put it down on the grass?'

'I expect we've got to learn how to work it,' Sheila told him. 'It would be dreadful if we got landed somewhere and couldn't get back.'

'Yes, we've got to think about that,' agreed Peter, 'let's all think now.'

The boat flew steadily on amid complete silence.

Suddenly Humphrey cried, 'Got it!' and leaped with excitement so that he nearly fell out and the others had to grab at his heels.

Three pairs of eyes were fixed anxiously upon him.

'You've got to *wish*!' Humphrey explained. Then seeing that they didn't understand, he went on, 'When Peter put it down at first he didn't wish, so nothing happened.'

'But he did wish,' Sheila reminded him; 'he said he wished it would take us anywhere.'

'But that wouldn't do. It was too—too sort of general. You have to wish—'

'A special place!' Sandy trumpeted.

'It wasn't until I said *Radcliff* that the thing began to work,' Peter agreed.

'What happens when we get there?' asked Sheila.

'Wait and see,' Peter advised.

It was lovely in the magic ship, lovelier than any one could possibly have imagined. The wind sent their hair streaming backwards. Birds flew past with movements scarcely less graceful than those of the ship. The children sang for joy in the keen, fresh air. The song that they sang had no words, it just came out in trills and rhythms because they were so happy.

'We can't fly right into Radcliff,' Sheila said suddenly, 'we'd be mobbed.'

'Besides, we don't know how to stop it properly; we might hurt some one,' said Humphrey.

'Let's stop about a mile out,' suggested Sandy.

Peter spoke clearly. 'Please stop in Farmer Pawson's meadow.'

'But not if there are any cows about,' added Sandy hastily.

The ship flew steadily on.

'We're nearly there,' said Peter after a time, feeling the boat slacken speed.

The earth seemed to float gently upwards with the movement that Peter was beginning to know. In a moment they were standing on the firm grass.

'Now, watch!' Peter commanded.

And Continues

They stood holding their breath while the flying-boat grew
smaller and smaller. Then they saw Peter pick it up and put
it in his pocket. The four children sat down in the high,
blossomy grass.

'What is it, Pete?' asked Sheila, noticing that his forehead
was wrinkling in the way it always did when he was troubled.

'Nothing!' said Peter shortly, and lay down with his face
buried in his hands.

'Fancy being broody when we've got a magic ship!'
exclaimed Sandy.

Humphrey said nothing. He knew what was bothering
Peter because it was beginning to bother him as well.

Peter lifted his worried face. 'I'm going to take it back,' he
said.

'Take *what* back?' asked Sheila and Sandy together.

Humphrey still said nothing. He knew what was coming.

'The ship,' Peter said in a low voice.

'Whatever *for*?' asked Sandy in amazement. But now
Sheila was beginning to understand, too.

'Because,' Peter explained, 'I've got to find out whether
the old chap *knew* it was magic when he sold it.'

'What difference does that make?' asked Sandy, who could
think of nothing but the disappointment of parting with the
wonderful ship.

'All the difference in the world. You see, magic doesn't
happen often—not once in a blue moon,' Sheila went on,
trying to get things clear. 'I expect there isn't another magic
ship like this in the whole world.'

'Well, what if there isn't?' demanded Sandy. 'It's Pete's.
He *paid* for it.'

19

'No, he didn't. Not what it's worth, anyhow,' Sheila went on. 'Why, it must be worth thousands and thousands, millions perhaps. It's the kind of thing a king might buy— King George perhaps.'

'Well, the princesses have got quite enough,' Sandy said firmly, 'and I don't see why they should have our ship!'

'That's not the point,' Humphrey explained. 'The point is that we think it was sold by mistake.'

'No one sells a magic ship for three shillings,' Peter said slowly. 'And he was an old man—poor. He was blind in one eye, too. He couldn't see properly.'

Sandy nodded gravely. Now that she understood she saw that the others were right.

'No time like the present,' said Peter, trying to make it sound joky, but not succeeding very well.

The four children stood up, brushing dry bits of grass from their clothes. Slowly and sadly they climbed over the gate and dropped down into the white road. Peter kept his hand inside his pocket, as if he wanted to feel the boat as long as he could. It comforted him a little. But not much.

They meant to walk briskly into Radcliff and get the horrid business over. *They meant to.* And yet every few minutes their feet slackened and dragged in the white dust of the road.

Peter said suddenly and fiercely because he was feeling so bad about everything, 'This won't do. It won't *do*! Look here, we'll race it!'

But though the race began well enough, no one had any heart for it. Presently they gave up all pretence and plodded on grimly. However, they hadn't very far to plod, because soon they were entering the crowded High Street that runs through Radcliff. Peter's fingers tightened on his boat, but he didn't say a word. His jaw, though, was pushed forward in the determined way they all knew.

He crossed over and turned to his left, and the others followed him. He walked a few steps, looked puzzled, and then walked back again. He walked several steps in the other direction, and the same thing happened. He tried again in the first direction, and then again in the second. He wandered backwards and forwards for about a quarter of an hour. At last he said, 'I can't find it.' And was ashamed of the happy feeling that sprang up in his heart.

The others said nothing, for Peter's chin was still thrust forward in warning.

'Nonsense,' he said, half to himself and half to the others, 'I can't find it because I don't want to find it. I'm not looking hard enough. It's *cheating*!'

Humphrey said, 'Why not go to Mr. Frinton's house and find the way from there?'

Peter nodded.

The four children all knew the way to Mr. Frinton's, and they stepped out briskly. In a few minutes they stood outside the house where the orange rambler swayed over and reflected its lovely self in Mr. Frinton's brass plate.

'Now!' said Sheila. And Sandy echoed, 'Now!'

Peter set off boldly in the direction he had taken earlier in the afternoon, and the others followed. But soon his steps slackened. He stood stock still. 'I can't find it!' he said.

'I know,' said Humphrey. 'Let's divide up and each take a

21

bit of the prom. We'll go up every turning in our bit and see if we can find Peter's street. We'll all meet by the bathing-huts in an hour's time.'

'We'll be awfully late for supper,' sighed Sandy.

'Who cares?' Peter asked scornfully, feeling that every mouthful would choke him until the fate of the magic ship was settled one way or another.

It was Humphrey who gave them their beats—Peter from the bathing-tents to the aquarium; Sheila from the aquarium to the bandstand; Sandy from the bandstand to the end of the Marina Hotel; and himself what was left.

Up and down went the children. Up streets and down streets. It took each child the full hour to search thoroughly. When they arrived at the meeting-place, the sky was dark blue and twinkling with stars. On the left the bandstand lights threw out winks of yellow and red and green. They could hear the soft, far-away sound of the music.

Peter's hand was still in his pocket stroking the little boat. They looked at each other inquiringly, then Sheila spoke.

'I think you were meant to keep it, Peter,' she said softly. 'I think that's part of the magic.'

Peter stood staring at her. Then his mouth widened into a smile. 'You're right, Sheila,' he said. 'I think so, anyhow. And it's not because I *want* to think it, either. You see, I've remembered something. He—the old man I mean—*knew* the value of it. He said all the money in the world wouldn't have bought it once. He said they didn't make ships like that nowadays, and that you had to pay all the money you had, and then a bit more. And so I did. Because I gave him father's twopence, too.'

'Then I *am* right, Peter,' Sheila said quietly. 'It was meant for you. It is yours.'

The four children stood very still for a moment; then quite suddenly, Peter leaped into the air crying, *'Hoorah, Hoorah!'*

When they had all finished cheering, Humphrey looked up at the dark sky. 'We ought to be back,' he said. 'They'll be awfully worried about us.'

'And now everything's settled, I want my supper. I'm starving!' announced Sandy.

Humphrey felt in his pocket and brought out a piece of toffee wrapped in paper. It was a bit sticky and a bit fluffy but Sandy wasn't proud and she accepted it with pleasure.

'We'll be home in a jiffy,' Peter promised. 'We'd better start her behind the breakwater where we shan't be seen.'

They pounded over the dark sand. Peter stooped under the shadow of the breakwater and drew the boat from his pocket. 'Home!' he whispered.

The boat began to grow in size. When it was large enough, the children stepped in.

If it had been fun before, sailing above the tree-tops in the daylight, it was far more wonderful now in the starry darkness. The moon poured her silver light on the flying-ship and upon the faces of the children within it. Sheila was sitting very still because a piece of poetry was making itself up in her head. Sandy was leaning against her, half-asleep, the toffee forgotten in her hand, and dreaming of supper. Humphrey was kneeling and looking over the side, thinking that the whole world drenched in silver was a marvellous map that had suddenly come alive.

But Peter stood upright at the prow with one arm round the golden neck of the boar.

CHAPTER 3

The First Adventure

Gertrude was waiting for them at the garden gate. They saw her as they ran down the cliff path, her cap and apron glimmering white in the darkness. Her face was rather white, too, but the children didn't notice that. She wanted to hug them when she saw them running swiftly down the path because they were back safe once more, but they had been out far too late and ought to be scolded instead.

'Wher*ever* have you been?' she asked in what she hoped was a scoldy sort of voice. But it couldn't have been very scoldy because Humphrey seized her arm and hugged it.

'Over the hills and far away!' he said softly.

'Go on with you!' cried Gertrude, trying to look severe but not succeeding very well. 'You're naughty children, yes, you are! All of you! You know very well you oughtn't to be out so late without asking first. And I'm very angry with you, yes, I am, and it's a good thing it's holidays and you can sleep longer to-morrow, and you don't deserve any supper, so there!'

'Oh!' said Sheila in a sorrowful sort of voice, and it wasn't of supper she was thinking.

'Oh!' cried Peter, and forgot in an instant his beloved ship.

'Oh!' said Humphrey, and turned away his face.

'Oh!' sighed Sandy, not feeling hungry any more, and hid her face in Gertrude's waist.

For suddenly they had remembered.

Supper-time was mother's time. Mother always came in at seven and said, 'Well, infants, what's for supper?' And she never forgot to ask, even though they always had the same thing.

Peter always had a handful of raisins, two chocolate biscuits (big ones), and a glass of lemonade (gassy).

Sheila always had two rounds of hot buttered toast with jam (rasp. or straw., but never, never blackcurrant because she couldn't bear it) and a cup of chocolate (not cocoa, because that is not at all the same thing).

Humphrey always had an orange, an apple, and a glass of lemonade made with lemon and lots of sugar.

Sandy always had rice crispies with golden syrup and a glass of milk and a banana.

But mother never forgot to ask them what they would like, though cook, I'm afraid, had got into the habit of getting the trays ready before the children had chosen. But you could hardly blame her for that. You or I or any one except the children's mother, would have done the same. But then, mother was mother, and quite, quite different from any one else.

But to-night there wouldn't be any mother to say, 'Well, infants, what's for supper?' Nor to-morrow night, nor for goodness knows how many nights. For mother was ill. And though no one had breathed a word about a nursing home, the children had seen Gertrude packing nightdresses and dressing-jackets and brushes and combs and toothbrushes, and all the things you take away with you. So it hadn't required a great deal of cleverness to guess where she was going—especially as it was not like mother to go away without saying good-bye. Besides, there was father wandering about with the most worried expression on his face.

Yes, they had been very unhappy indeed, but then with all the excitement of Peter going into Radcliff by himself, and the magic boat and everything, it had all gone out of their mind. And now the worry had come back again, and nothing, not even the magic boat itself, seemed to matter very much.

They walked quietly up the garden path, Sandy dabbing at her eyes in the darkness. Sheila went straight through the hall and upstairs.

'I'm going to bed,' she said in a choky sort of voice, standing in the middle of the staircase. 'I don't want any supper.'

'Nor me!' said Peter.

'Nor me!' echoed Humphrey and Sandy.

Gertrude stood at the foot of the stairs to prevent the others from following Sheila.

'You go straight into the dining-room,' she said, trying to look as fierce as a turkey-cock, but only succeeding in looking like a fluffed-out sparrow. 'I've promised your mother I'd look after you the same as if she was here, and I mean to do it!' And she hustled them into the dining-room.

It was cosy in there with the curtains drawn. The four little trays stood on the table looking as jolly as ever. It was difficult to believe that mother wouldn't come in any minute.

Sheila's tray was yellow, and the china was yellow with white spots.

Peter's was grass-green with white spots.

Humphrey's was sky-blue with white spots.

And Sandy's was deep rose-pink with white spots.

Mother had brought them each a set from Italy last year, and very pretty they looked.

Gertrude said, 'Get on with it, do! It's ever so late. Miss. Sheila will be down in a minute.'

Peter stared down into his green tumbler, watching the tiny bubbles rise and break on the surface. 'The gas will soon be fizzed out,' he said, and lifted the tumbler to his lips.

'Better for you without gas,' said Humphrey, and reached out for the sky-blue tray.

Sandy said nothing. She was already working the syrup amongst the rice crispies and admiring it as it glistened like gold on the pink plate.

Gertrude didn't waste much time upstairs, for presently Sheila came down looking a little red about the eyes, but quite cheerful. She lifted the chocolate-skin on her spoon and set it down neatly on the yellow saucer.

The children ate and drank steadily, and felt better for their supper. Then Sheila said, 'You nip up first, Sandy, and don't take all the water!'

'It's Huff's turn to go up first,' objected Sandy.

'No, it isn't. I went up first last night.'

'Well, it's a shame!' Sandy was pouting. 'Why have Huff and I always got to have our baths at night? Why can't we have them in the morning like you and Peter?'

28

'Because you've got to go to bed clean,' Sheila explained.

'Catch *you* getting up half an hour earlier for a bath!' grinned Peter.

'No arguing!' Sheila declared firmly. 'Up you go, Sandy. And Huff's coming up in a quarter of an hour. And if you're not out, we'll come and drag you out!'

'Pooh!' said Sandy. But she went quite quickly.

Sheila was standing by her bedroom window. She was feeling fresh and bright after a quick cold wash, and now, standing there and brushing her hair, with the fresh breeze coming up from the garden, she didn't feel in the least bit like going to sleep. Sandy lay curled up in bed, one plump arm thrown up over the pillow. The bedclothes trailed over the floor.

Sheila went over and, picking them up, folded them neatly over the foot of the bed.

'Too hot!' she told herself. 'Mother would have taken off a blanket.' And at the thought of mother, the tears came pricking into her eyes. Sleep seemed more impossible than ever. She came over to the window again and, dropping on her knees, put her elbows on the broad ledge. From the garden came a dozen sweet smells.

Sheila closed her eyes and wondered whether she could distinguish them. She was quite sure she could smell roses and night-scented stock.

She sniffed. Lime or honeysuckle? She couldn't be quite sure. But she was certain of the tobacco-plant, it had such a strong and heavy perfume. She sniffed again. A quite different smell of tobacco told her that father was coming down the garden-path. Yes, father, and with him another man. She stared intently into the darkness. The other man was Uncle David.

They came on steadily and underneath Sheila's window they stopped. There was a wooden garden-seat just there and the two men sat down.

They were still talking, and Sheila went on hiding in the darkness. She was thinking that the minute they stopped she would call out quietly and ask if there was any news of mother.

Father and Uncle David went on talking. And Sheila went on waiting. She saw Uncle David get up and put a hand on father's shoulder. And then, quite suddenly, she understood that they were speaking of mother.

Sheila's heart gave a sudden sickening drop.

'Seems queer it all coming on so suddenly,' said Uncle David. 'I don't seem to have got used to the idea yet.'

'That sort of trouble often comes with a rush,' father said drearily. 'You know, David, she'd be all right if she'd only give herself a chance. But she won't. It's the children. She keeps worrying about the children—'

'Well, why can't she see them?' asked Uncle David.

Father shrugged. 'Not allowed. The surgeon says she's not strong enough and it would upset everything. I don't agree, though, I think it would do her good.'

'Well,' said Uncle David reasonably, 'after all, the surgeon knows best.'

'No he doesn't,' father said in his most determined sort of

voice. 'I know best. Because I know Mary better than any one else. If she wants to see the children she'll fret herself sick until she does. And the minute she's seen them she'll settle down and get better.'

Sheila didn't hear any more because father got up quickly and walked away.

She went over and sat on her bed. She wanted to think. From the other bed came the sound of Sandy's soft regular breathing. She sat perfectly still, trying to make up her mind.

The other doctor had said No, but father said Yes. Father loved mother best in the whole world and father said Yes.

She got off the bed, crept along the passage and pushed open the door of the boys' room.

'Peter,' she called gently, and then a little louder, 'Peter!'

Peter lay fast asleep with one hand under the pillow where the magic boat lay. She went up and touched him gently on the shoulder. He came awake immediately, his fingers tightening round his treasure.

'Listen, Peter,' she said in quick urgent whispers, and she told him what she had overheard from the window.

Peter sat up in bed and stared at her, his face very white in the moonlight. He couldn't bear to think that mother was so ill. He couldn't bear to think that she was wanting and wanting them and couldn't get better without them. It was like a pain in the middle of his chest. He felt he would do anything to help mother get better, anything at all. He felt little and powerless to do anything. He buried his face in the pillow so that Sheila shouldn't see his distress.

Something moved under the pillow, moved like a bird. Peter sat up again in the moonlight. He was smiling.

31

He said, 'We'll go and see mother, all of us. Let's wake the others.' And then very anxiously, 'You're sure we ought to go, *sure?*'

She nodded. 'I'm going to wake Sandy.'

Sandy didn't understand at first. She was having a very satisfactory dream about a flying-boat that was made of pink peppermint rock. But when at last she did understand, she put on her dressing-gown and then sat down in the moonlight to put on her slippers.

Humphrey came awake at once. He understood the minute he opened his eyes, because this was, in a way, continuing his dream. He had been dreaming of mother. He had been dreaming that he was a bird flying across the sky straight to mother.

Sandy came into the boys' room tying the girdle of her dressing-gown and the three children sat on Peter's bed and waited for him to speak.

'We're going to see mother, now, this very minute. I don't know if the ship will take off from a room but we're going to try.'

'Oughtn't the children to be properly dressed?' asked Sheila a little anxiously.

'Who's going to waste time dressing when mother wants us?' asked Peter. 'And what's the matter with dressing-gowns? And anyhow it's as warm as toast.'

'Hot or cold toast?' asked Sandy, who was always interested in food.

But none of the others even heard her.

Peter put the magic ship in the middle of the floor.

It looked incredibly tiny lying there on its side. Staring at it, the children wondered whether the adventures of the day were not all a dream—and whether, even now, they were not in the middle of some dream.

'But we don't know where mother is,' Humphrey said at last.

'I don't think that matters,' Peter replied. He went over and put his hand on the head of the golden boar. 'Please take us to mother,' he said.

The four children fixed their eyes on the boat.

Was it growing, really and truly growing? Or were they only imagining it because they wanted it to happen so much? They could hardly breathe with excitement. Suddenly, Sheila was sure. She went over and threw open the window as wide as it would go.

The four children stepped inside the boat. It raised itself gently from the carpet and nosed towards the window. As they went through Humphrey stretched out his hand and caught at a bunch of rambler roses that nodded against the wall. In a moment they were sailing up into the star-pricked sky.

The boat flew steadily onwards. After a while the children felt it slacken and sink. Down, down went the boat, and settled as gently as a moth. The children stepped out on to a wide veranda. They stood silently until the boat was no more than a toy, hardly to be seen in the shadows of the veranda. Then Peter picked it up and put it in his pyjama pocket.

Right in front of them rose the bulk of the high dark house. Here and there a window shone yellow where a light had been left burning.

'I wonder which is mother's room?' whispered Sheila, and tip-toed in the shadow trying to find out. The window of a softly shaded room opened on to the veranda and Sheila crept towards it. Very stealthily she peeped inside, and then, with uplifted finger, she beckoned the others.

Holding their breath, the four children stared in.

It was mother lying in the narrow white bed, but a mother they hardly knew, with her bandaged head and no smile on her pale face. A nurse stood by the bed, her cap and apron very white in the dim glow. She was speaking, and the children could just catch her words.

'Try to sleep, Mrs. Grant,' she was saying. 'You've simply *got* to give yourself a chance to get better!'

Mother answered, but in so low a voice that the children could not hear what she said. But the nurse replied briskly, 'You shall see them as soon as you're well enough. That's a promise! Now you must do your bit by trying to settle down for the night. That's the first step to getting well!'

She smoothed the already smooth pillow and drew the neat quilt a tiny bit straighter. 'I'll just put your flowers out for the night,' she said, and stepped out on to the veranda.

Would she step to the right or to the left? If to the left, she would step straight into the middle of the children. They crouched flattened against the wall of the house.

She came out humming a little tune under her breath. She glanced sharply to the left as if a little uneasy, and then moved towards a little cane table that stood on the right. Having set down the flowers, she stood for a moment looking over the quiet, dark garden. Then she went inside again, leaving the veranda window ajar.

34

Sheila, watching, saw her stop for a second by the bed and then disappear, closing the door gently behind her.

The four children looked anxiously at each other. Crouched flat against the wall, Peter whispered, 'Ought we to go in?'

'It's what we've come for!' Sandy reminded him in as low a voice.

'She looks awfully ill,' Humphrey said slowly, 'we might upset her or something.'

Sheila wrinkled her forehead and said nothing. It was her idea, and she felt responsible. Absently she whistled a tune, it was a trick she had when she was thinking deeply. It was their favourite tune *Bobby Shaftoe*. Mother had sung it to them hundreds of times.

Watching, the children saw mother raise herself very slowly and carefully in bed and look steadily towards the window. It was as if she was looking straight at them in the darkness. She was smiling, and in spite of the bandage she was once more the mother they knew.

'Children,' she whispered, 'Where are you? I know you're there. Come in, oh, *do* come in!'

Sheila pushed open the window and tiptoed up to the bed. The others followed, making no sound in the quiet room.

'Darlings!' said mother, and lay back smiling on the pillow.

Sheila said, 'Mother darling, we oughtn't to be here at all, but we wanted to see you terribly badly.'

'You mustn't worry about us,' Peter said, 'because we're managing ever so well, honest we are!'

'We had our suppers just the same as usual,' Sandy said.

'Good!' murmured mother in her weak voice.

'I thought you'd like to know!' Sandy added.

Mother smiled feebly.

'But we all want you to get well quickly as quickly,' Sheila said earnestly, 'and come back to us the first minute you can.'

Humphrey said nothing. There was nothing he could say because his throat felt choky. But he went right close to the bed and laid his cluster of roses on mother's pillow.

She turned her head and smelled them. Her eyelids drooped over her tired eyes.

Sheila led the others to the window. 'Good-bye, mother darling,' she said. But mother didn't answer. Her eyes were closed and her gentle breathing told them that she was fast asleep.

Outside on the veranda Peter took the boat from his pocket. 'Home!' he said.

Flying swiftly homewards, Sheila said, 'I wonder whether she'll think it was a dream.'

'I expect so,' Peter said, 'but it doesn't really matter, the only thing that matters is that she's gone off to sleep.'

'There are the roses,' thought Humphrey, and said nothing.

Sandy, too, said nothing. She lay curled up at the bottom of the homeward-flying boat fast asleep.

'I saw them,' mother kept repeating the next morning. 'I saw them as clearly as I see you!'

The First Adventure

A dream! Nurse's face said as clearly as a face could speak. 'Of course the children came,' said mother answering the look. 'I don't know how, but I wanted them and there they were. Besides—there are the roses.'

CHAPTER 4

The Land of the Nile

The children were in the playroom. Peter was frowning over his book, Sheila was knitting something that she hoped would turn into a jumper when it was finished, Humphrey was absorbed in a jig-saw puzzle of the world, and Sandy was tidying her own particular cupboard in the hope of finding an odd sweet or two that might have slipped down a crack.

Suddenly Peter closed his book with a bang. 'Who cares a bean about *The Land of the Pyramids*?' he demanded crossly.

Sheila looked up and dropped a stitch. 'Why on earth should you?' she asked.

'We've got to write an essay on Egypt this term. Holiday work! School to-morrow and I haven't read a word. And I don't want to, either!'

Humphrey fitted a piece carefully into his puzzle. Then he looked up. 'Let's go to Egypt and find out something about it,' he suggested.

'Jolly good idea!' exclaimed Peter, and banged his book on the table.

'Do! Oh let's!' cried Sheila, dropping her knitting.

Sandy glanced up at the cuckoo-clock on the wall. 'It's nearly lunch time,' she said, picking some fluff off an acid-drop she had discovered.

'Greedy little pig!' cried Peter. 'It's only eleven. Look here, Huff, go down and ask cook to pack us something nice for lunch. She'll do it for you! She likes you best, heaven knows why! Still, there's no accounting for tastes. Tell her we're off for the day. Tell her the weather's too gorgeous to be wasted. Tell her we're going back to school to-morrow. Tell her she's the darling of your heart, tell her whatever you like, only go!' And he pushed a somewhat bewildered Humphrey out of the door.

In two minutes Humphrey's beaming face reappeared.

'She says all right!' he announced.

'What's she going to give us?' asked Sandy with great interest.

'Wait and see!' Humphrey told her. 'Gertrude says she'll bring up the parcels in a quarter of an hour.'

Sheila wound up her wool, stuck the needles carefully through the ball, and put it away in her workbag.

Sandy, after looking to see whether yet another acid-drop might not be hidden in a dark corner, cleared up by the simple method of flinging everything back into the cupboard and shutting the door.

Humphrey went off to find a handkerchief because he thought it might be a useful sort of thing to have if he was going to be out for the whole day.

Peter took up the flying-boat and rubbed lovingly at its wooden sides with an old silk scarf.

Presently Gertrude's kind face appeared in the doorway. Four brown-paper parcels dangled from her fingers.

'Here you are,' she said. 'Have a good time and make the most of your day and don't get into mischief.'

She put the parcels down on the table and came over to where Peter stood polishing the boat.

'Pretty isn't it?' she said admiringly.

'It'll take you over the hills and far away!' Humphrey said.

'You said that once before,' Gertrude answered laughing. 'You take care I don't keep you to your word one day!' And she gave his arm a little squeeze as she went by.

'Well, who's ready?' asked Peter as the door closed behind her.

'Me! Me!! Me!!!' cried three voices together.

'Start her off from the cove?' Peter asked, and the others nodded.

It was lovely down on the beach. The sand was hot and wet and ribbed, and there was a gentle breeze blowing. Away at the edge of the sand, the waves were lazily crawling, tipped white with foam. But the children did not even look at the sea, they could think of nothing but the adventure before them.

In the shelter of their favourite cove, Peter took out the ship and put it down on the firm sand.

'Egypt!' he said.

The four children knelt down and stared with never-failing wonder at the miracle. They could never quite believe it really would happen.

But it did happen and they clambered aboard. It was keen high up in the sky, and the boat tossed a little in the light wind. But presently the wind dropped and the boat flew steadily on. Kneeling over the gunwale, Humphrey was soon lost in the delightful pastime of seeing the country-side spread like a living map beneath them. Sandy was wondering what cook had put in their parcels and Sheila and Peter were standing together at the golden prow and chatting about what they meant to do.

'Pyramids!' cried Sheila.

'Temples!' exclaimed Peter who had heard about them at school.

'Alexandria!' whispered Humphrey still looking downwards. 'Or Cairo. Or Memphis.'

'A bazaar!' said Sandy happily. 'We could buy some Egyptian sweets.'

'We all seem to want something different,' said Peter, 'Let's leave it to the ship.'

He bent over and stroked the golden boar. 'Anywhere in Egypt,' he said.

It seemed to Peter that the golden boar nodded wisely. Or perhaps it was only the effect of the sunshine streaming across the prow.

Up went the ship.

'Lotus lilies,' said Sheila. 'I shall make a wreath for my hair.'

'Pyramids and mummies,' said Peter. 'I shall find a heap of gold and jewels and make all our fortunes.'

'Floods and rice fields,' said Humphrey. 'I wish they'd let me see how irrigation works.'

'Funny things to eat,' said Sandy. 'I wonder what they'll taste like!'

The ship held a steady course. A cold wind whistled through their hair and the two girls buttoned up their cardigans. They looked downwards and there was the grey and choppy sea spread beneath them. Below the magic boat gulls dipped and soared with the sunlight slanting over their white wings.

'The Channel!' said Humphrey. 'Gosh, if we should fall out!'

'Rather a high dive!' grinned Peter and grabbed him by the shoulder. Sheila put a protecting arm round Sandy's waist.

Far below them, a cross-Channel steamer, looking no larger than the tiniest toy, ploughed across the water, leaving a long trail of white in its wake.

The flying-boat held its course so swiftly that in a little while the steamer was no more than a black speck on the grey water.

Suddenly Humphrey cried, 'Land!' and the others crowded to his side of the boat. The white cliffs of France swung into view.

'We're flying across France—and then which way, I wonder?' said Humphrey thoughtfully. 'I wish the ship would drop a little so we could see things!'

Immediately the ship began to drop.

Soon the soft, somewhat hazy, colours of the landscape, began to sharpen and deepen.

'Look!' cried Sheila pointing to a grove of low, grey, twisted trees. 'Olives!'

'Who cares?' said Sandy. 'Nasty bitter things, worse than medicine.'

Presently the sea lay beneath them once more, only now it was blue as turquoise, with scarcely a ripple to break its glassy surface.

'The Mediterranean,' sighed Humphrey happily.

'Look, there's Sicily,' cried Sheila. 'I can see Vesuvius. Look, look, I believe it's smoking!'

'Etna!' corrected Humphrey. 'Vesuvius is near Naples.'

'And anyhow that's smoke coming from a steamer,' added Peter.

'Oh dear,' sighed Sheila. 'How disappointing! A real live volcano is so romantic.'

'That depends how near you are to it,' grinned Peter.

'Good-bye Greece!' cried Humphrey, leaning over the side and waving his hand.

'Where?' asked Sandy rushing round.

'Too late,' said Humphrey.

'The sea's getting bluer and bluer,' cried Sheila. 'It's like the sapphire in mother's ring.'

The ship held its course over the brilliant blue sea. Now and again, an island small and brilliant as a jewel swung into sight and then away again.

'Look!' cried Peter suddenly, 'I believe we're coming to land!'

The others looked eagerly in the direction of his pointing finger. At first there was nothing to be seen but a cloud low down on the horizon. Gradually it hardened into flat roofs topped by water cisterns.

'Not much to see!' said Sandy, staring down at the huddle of low houses staining the blue sky with smoke.

'Wait a minute!' cried Peter. 'That must have been the old part of the town. Look we're coming to the new bit now!'

'Gosh, what a city!' exclaimed Humphrey as the ship sped

swiftly over a great and busy town. Modern stream-lined buildings took the sun on their plate-glass windows. Even at that distance the children could see motors, like insects, speeding along the white road.

'Might almost be London,' remarked Sheila. 'Except for the colours! Did you ever *see* such blue and white and gold?'

'Cairo, I suppose,' said Humphrey. 'I wish I knew, though!'

Now they were flying over a level plain and the children could see that it was richly cultivated, although they could not make out the crops. Here and there rose dark brown mounds of ancient cities. Everywhere the shapely fans of palm trees cut into the fierce blue sky. Now the rich fertile plain seemed to shrink gradually, and now they were flying above a strip of brilliant green, winding like a ribbon through the heart of the desert which lay glowing and golden on either side.

'The brightest green in the world!' said Sandy.

'The valley of the Nile,' Humphrey said softly, 'and look, oh look, there's the Nile itself.'

The children hung breathless, staring down at the dark green water.

'Must be full of crocodiles,' said Sandy shivering.

East and west stretched the great desert. Here and there, bare yellow rock stood like solid sunlight against the incredible blue of the sky.

'I could go on flying like this for ever,' said Peter.

'I couldn't. I'm hungry,' Sandy said firmly.

The boat began to drop slowly. The green earth rose to

meet them. With a long gliding movement, it slid down by the river.

'Good old boar!' Peter said, affectionately throwing one arm round the neck of the golden boar. 'Well, what now?'

'Lunch!' said Sandy at once.

'Rather!' agreed Sheila. 'Flying gives me an appetite.'

They unpacked their parcels and spread out the contents.

'Good!' said Peter.

'Good!' said Sheila.

'Good!' said Humphrey.

Sandy said nothing. She was far too busy.

This is what cook had packed.

Tongue and chicken sandwiches. A big pile. Without mustard. Four nice round tomatoes, the firm kind that don't squelch when you bite into them.

Four sausage rolls.

Four small cream cheeses wrapped in silver paper.

Four large crispy chocolate biscuits.

Four large juicy Jaffa oranges, the kind you can peel easily.

For some time there was absolute silence near the river.

After a while, Sandy sat back and picked the crumbs from her lap. Then because she didn't believe in waste, she popped them in her mouth, and smiled round at the others.

'Cook's a trump,' said Peter.

'If I find a gold crown,' said Humphrey dreamily, 'I shall give it to cook.'

'I don't think a crown would suit her exactly,' remarked Sandy, trying to imagine cook's red face under a golden crown.

'Now children, no arguing,' said Sheila briskly. 'What are we going to do?'

'The bazaar,' said Sandy very quickly. 'It's my choose, because I said it first.'

'All right,' Peter agreed. He scrambled to his feet. 'There's such a lot of things to do, don't let's waste any time.'

Sheila said thoughtfully, 'I don't think we ought to take the magic ship with us. We might lose it, there must be lots and lots of pickpockets about in bazaars.'

'No worse than anywhere else, I expect,' said Peter, who didn't like parting with his ship even for a moment.

'Worse for us if we can't get home again,' Humphrey reminded him.

'If we lost the ship,' added Sandy, turning quite pale, 'it would be *awful*!'

'Well, what ought we to do?' Peter asked unhappily.

'Hide it,' Sheila suggested.

'We mightn't find it again,' said Sandy.

'We'd mark the place, silly!' Humphrey told her.

'Do you really think we ought to hide it?' asked Peter, still troubled.

'Honest, I do!' said Humphrey, and Sheila nodded.

'All right,' said Peter at last.

'Now that's settled,' remarked Sandy, 'let's find the bazaar.'

Peter took the ship out of his pocket. 'To a bazaar,' he said, 'and please stop a bit of the way outside the town.'

The ship rose into the air.

'There's the town,' cried Peter, pointing to his right. And

indeed it was plain to see, with the blue smoke rising from the low houses, with here and there a great dome curving white against the deep sky.

Now the ship was floating gently above the green ribbon of the Nile. Every now and again the children could see brown Egyptian backs and straw-shaded hats bent low over the young rice. And sometimes a brown face would lift itself from its work to stare at the strange bright bird flying above in the hot blue sky, such a bird as they had never seen before.

At last the ship slowed down, sank gently, and brought them to land in an empty spot a couple of miles from the city gates.

'Now let's hide it,' said Sheila as they stood watching the ship grow smaller.

The children looked round. It was not an ideal spot for hiding anything. In that smooth sandy stretch one place was too like another. Then Sheila's quick eye caught sight of a half-buried block of stone. 'Here!' she said.

Peter knelt down and dug in the sand with his fingers. He pushed the boat into the shallow hole and covered it up again, blowing the sand over the marks his fingers had made. Then he stood up, carefully measuring the distance from the stone with his eye.

'I don't like leaving it,' he said a little troubled.

'Much better than having it pinched, honest, it is!' Humphrey reminded him, and Sheila nodded in agreement.

The four children set off along the hot and dusty road.

CHAPTER 5

Adventure in a Bazaar

The road was quite empty at first except for themselves, but in ones and twos at first, and then in little groups of threes and fours, more and more people thronged the road. They were dressed in flowing robes of cotton, with long wide sleeves almost sweeping the sand of the road. Each man wore a scarlet fez upon his head, and the women were, for the most part, veiled. Their brilliant dark eyes stared over the white folds of their filmy veils, in surprise at these white children who wandered alone, with no grown-up to guard them. The scarlet fezzes standing like tiny towers upon the smooth blue-black heads, the nut-brown faces and the wide flowing robes of dazzling blue and white, made the children feel that an exciting adventure had begun.

And indeed it had! But quite how exciting they were not to guess. If they had, perhaps they would not have stepped along the road quite so gaily.

At the city gate the crowd of people was so dense that the children, flattened against the wall, had to wait their turn. It was bewildering—the bright colours and the brown faces in the brilliant sunshine, and the flash of white teeth, and the meaningless chatter of high foreign voices; the tinkle of camel-bells as the tall, swaying beasts picked their delicate way, the braying of asses, the neighing of horses, the pip-pip of motors, the pinging of bicycles, and the rattle of native carts.

At last they managed to squeeze their way in through the gate. The street in which they found themselves was narrow and noisy but full of gay colour. Full of smells, too! Above them blazed the deep blue sky with a sun like brass. The two girls unbuttoned their cardigans.

'I wonder where the bazaar is?' asked Sandy.

'If we follow the crowd we're bound to get there, sooner or later,' Sheila answered.

The four children marched steadily on. They were aware that they were attracting a good deal of attention and it made them a little uncomfortable. For the first time in their lives they almost wished that they had some grown-up with them.

At last they found themselves in the centre of the town. A long covered walk whose white, rough-cast roof was supported by pillars, stood in front of them, its shadow bright blue upon the yellow ground.

'Thank heaven for a bit of shade,' said Peter, pushing the damp hair back from his forehead. He squeezed his way through the crowd passing between the pillars, and the others followed him.

It was dim and confusing after the brilliant sunshine outside, and for a time the children could see nothing. After a little while they could make out the little dark booths and the stalls piled high with gay merchandise.

'Oh!' cried Sheila, stopping to gaze at a piece of bright orange silk, but Sandy tugged at her arm.

'The sweet stalls are just across there!' she cried.

But the others did not even hear. They were staring with all their might at the flower-market, where roses of all colours, white and yellow jasmine, geraniums of crimson and pink and white, rosy oleanders and scarlet poinsettias were heaped in a glorious riot of colour. Even Sandy stopped for a moment, then she tugged again at Sheila's arm. The two boys cast a regretful look behind, where a juggler was spreading his mat, but since it was Sandy's turn to choose, and since she was so impatient, they followed her to the sweet-market.

Sandy stopped short in front of a low stall. Little brass dishes of queer-looking mixtures stood temptingly set out. The owner of the stall was at their side in a moment, his dark face wreathed in smiles, his hands waving in the air. He and the four children stood staring at each other in silence, then he thrust his face close to Sheila's and said something rapidly in his own tongue.

'Pardong?' said Sheila who had heard that French was much spoken in Egypt. But it was clear that this man had no use for French. So Peter tried. 'No savvy,' he remarked, having heard that this was always a useful sort of thing to say. But this was no use either. Another man, just as dark and excited, darted out of the little dark shop behind the stall, and joined the first. They were so ridiculously alike that they might have been twins. Now both men were talking excitedly at the tops of their voices, and waving their hands wildly at the children. To add to their difficulties, a crowd was collecting.

Peter was beginning to be worried. After all, he was the eldest and he had brought the others here. He had seen quite enough of the bazaar, he thought. It was close and smelly and the bright sun had given him a headache, and he didn't like the way the brown-skinned men were behaving. It was awkward not being able to speak a word to them. The best thing, Peter thought, would be to get back through the crowd, back to the magic ship and home. England, with its grey seas and its cool sunshine and its people who understood what you were saying, was suddenly very dear to him.

He clutched hold of Sheila with one hand and Sandy with the other. 'Keep close!' he whispered, and began to work his way through the crowd. But the crowd pressed inwards so that the children could not escape, they stood helplessly in the narrow space between the stall and the onlookers.

The men were fingering their little brass bowls and holding them out to the children.

'He's offering us some of his sweets,' whispered Sandy.

'It looks like it,' Peter agreed.

'I don't think mother would like us to take sweets from strangers,' remarked Sheila doubtfully.

'They're trying to be friendly,' explained Humphrey. 'Wouldn't it be rather rude to refuse?'

'It would be *very* rude!' answered Sandy quickly. 'Mother would simply hate us to be rude.' And she held out her hand.

The brown man lifted one of his brass basins from the stall and handed it to her with a bow. Inside there was something that looked like putty. The children stared at it a little doubtfully.

'Looks queer!' whispered Peter.

Sandy took a pinch between her finger and thumb and put it in her mouth.

'Lovely!' she said and held out the basin to the others.

It *was* lovely.

'Whatever is it made of?' said Humphrey, licking the crumbs from his lips into his mouth.

'Almonds I should think!' said Sheila. 'It's like marzipan, only much softer.'

'It's crispy, too!' said Peter.

'Honey I should think,' said Sandy and reached out for some more.

Quite soon the bowl was empty and the stall-holder held out another.

'Sugared rose-petals,' said Sheila peeping and shaking her head.

The crowd round the children grew denser from minute to minute.

The two men held out bowl after bowl. The children peered inside trying to guess what each held. 'Preserved ginger!' said Sandy.

'Sugared figs!' said Sheila.

'Turkish Delight!' said Peter.

Bowl after bowl was lifted down from the stall. At first the children tasted a little here and there, but soon they shook their heads, smiling.

'Thank you very much,' Peter said politely, forgetting that they could not understand him, 'we must be going now.'

He turned away, but the first man caught him by the

collar. He was speaking rapidly in his own language and he was not smiling quite so widely.

Peter shook his head.

The smile had now completely vanished. There was a rumbling, grumbling sort of murmur from the crowd that didn't sound comforting. The man came very near and clawed at Sandy's arm. Peter thought that the hand looked like a paw on her white woollen coat.

'You leave my sister alone!' he said loudly to show that he wasn't afraid, and he caught at Sandy's other arm. The man began to make even more excited gestures. He waved his hands wildly in the air. He dropped Sandy's arm and came over pointing to Peter's pocket.

'He only wants to be paid,' Humphrey said cheerfully, 'come on, Sandy, stump up!'

'I can't. I haven't any money!' whispered Sandy.

'*What!*' cried the others in horror.

'Well, why should I have, any more than you?' asked Sandy ready to cry.

'Didn't you keep talking about the bazaar?' demanded Peter.

'And the sweets you were going to buy?' asked Sheila.

'Of course we thought you had the money to buy them with,' added Humphrey.

'It isn't my fault,' sobbed Sandy, 'you oughtn't to go on adventures without money. You're older than me, anyhow!'

'So we oughtn't. And so we are!' exclaimed Humphrey suddenly. 'And anyhow it's no good blaming any one. What we've got to do is to find a way out of this fix.'

And now the crowd sounded noisier than ever. The grumbling began to take on an ugly sound. A stone just missed Peter and fell with a clatter against a brass bowl.

Peter went white to the lips.

'What is happening?' The deep foreign voice rose clear above the excited chatter. The crowd gave way and a tall figure clothed in a European suit of dazzling white, and wearing a scarlet fez, stood facing the children. The stall-holders bowed repeatedly, spreading out their hands, but he turned his back upon them.

'What is the matter?' he asked, and the children's hearts leaped to hear their own language. It sounded a little different—a little foreign, more musical perhaps, but they were overjoyed to know that here was some one who could understand them and whom they could understand.

Peter looked up at the dark bronze face, with its deep-set eyes and full proud lips.

'We've eaten his sweets and we haven't any money to pay for them,' he said blushing crimson.

'You see,' Sheila stammered, 'we didn't understand what they were saying. We thought they were inviting us. We thought they were being *awfully* polite.'

The stranger's mouth parted in a smile. 'Well now you *do* understand,' he said, and his teeth were very white in his dark face, 'Why do you not pay?'

'It was all my fault,' said Sandy, blinking back the tears. She hunted in her cardigan for a handkerchief, but it must have fallen overboard. The stranger took a clean unfolded handkerchief of finest linen from the pocket of his crisp white suit and handed it to Sandy with a deep bow.

'And why was it your fault?' he asked.

'Because,' Sandy said, 'I told the others I was going to buy sweets. I *kept* telling them, and I forgot about money.'

The stranger turned to the owners of the stall and said a few words in their own language. Then he pulled some silver from his pocket and threw it down upon the board. The money jingled and hopped and the two men darted to pick it up. The stranger turned and, bowing, offered one arm to Sandy and the other to Sheila who felt very grown up indeed as she slipped her arm in his.

They stepped forward and the crowd vanished as quickly as it had come—but a good deal more quietly. With a little girl on either arm, and the two boys pressing close behind, the stranger strode forward while the stall-holders followed, bowing repeatedly and spreading their hands.

Walking through the hot sunshine, the stranger said, 'I do not remember to have seen you before, yet four English children in so small a town are not to be missed. I think we should introduce ourselves.' He removed the scarlet fez from his glossy black hair.

'Ali Suleiman Ferouz at your service.'

'How do you do, sir?' asked Peter shaking hands. 'This is my sister Sheila. This is Sandy. This is Humphrey, and I'm Peter, Peter Grant.'

'Well, my friends,' said Ali Suleiman Ferouz, putting on his fez again, 'I am pleased to meet you. I am puzzled, however, because I do not remember to have seen you before, nor to have heard your names. When did you arrive?'

'This afternoon,' Peter replied.

'That is impossible, unless indeed, you came by private plane, and even then I should have known. Tell me,' he fixed a piercing eye upon Peter, 'how did you come?'

'We flew,' said Peter, hoping that the questions would now stop.

But it was Sandy who asked the next one.

'Why should you have known? Do you know every one who arrives?'

'But of course,' their new friend assured them. 'I am governor of this town. It is not a large town, I grant you, but it is important, because of its position.'

'What's the name of it?' asked Humphrey, always eager for new information.

'Ferouza.'

'Like your own name!' exclaimed Sandy.

Ali Suleiman Ferouz bowed. 'My family have been princes and guardians of Ferouza for hundreds of years.'

'*Princes!*' stammered Sandy, her eyes goggling with excitement. 'Oh, Your Majesty!'

'Highness,' whispered Sheila. 'You only say *Majesty* to the king!' Oh dear me, she was thinking, a real live prince! Whatever will happen next? It's awfully romantic. The girls at school will never believe me when I tell them. Perhaps I'd better *not* tell them!

'Well, my young friends,' said the prince, 'what can I do for you?' He glanced down at Sandy who was clinging to his hand.

'The young lady looks weary,' he suggested.

'I am a bit, Your Majesty—I mean Your Royal Highness,' replied Sandy. 'And I'm hungry, too.'

'That is a pity,' exclaimed the prince. 'But at least you need not be hungry long. Will you not all come to my house to rest and to refresh yourselves.'

'It's very kind of you,' Peter said a little doubtfully, 'but—'

'Well, that is settled, is it not?'

As they passed through the city gates the crowd parted, bowing respectfully. Outside, a long cream-coloured Hispanio-Suiza stood waiting. A chauffeur in native dress sprang to attention. Soon they were racing down the hot and shadeless road.

In a few moments the car stopped with a long gliding movement, and the dark-faced white-clad chauffeur sprang to the door. A high wall went up sheer before them. At a low gate two soldiers stood smartly to attention. The children passed through between the saluting soldiers and found themselves in a shady courtyard cooled by fountains and sweet-smelling shrubs. Acacias hung their purple tassels against the white walls; the scent of lilies was heavy about them. The water was tossed upwards into the hot quivering air in thousands upon thousands of diamond drops. In the basin of the fountain floated the royal flower, the blue lotus. The children stood staring down at the beautiful blooms floating in the jade-green water. Then they followed their new friend inside.

'Fancy having tea in a real palace,' whispered Sandy.

'It's awfully romantic,' Sheila whispered back again.

'I wonder what they'll give us to eat,' said Sandy clasping her two hands over her stomach.

'Oh, shut up!' said Peter crossly. He was worried without exactly knowing why. 'If it hadn't been for you, we shouldn't—'

'Have been here,' Sandy finished.

'And I'm not sure how wise that is!' thought Peter, though he said nothing.

Ali Suleiman Ferouz clapped his hands. Instantly a servant appeared in flowing white garments. The prince turned to his visitors. 'What may I have the pleasure of ordering for you?' he asked.

'Something cold to drink, if you please,' said Humphrey.

'Something to eat, please,' said Sandy, smiling up at her new friend.

'I don't think we ought to trouble you, really,' said Peter, who was not as happy as the others.

The inside of the palace was as magnificent as the outside. The great room was hung with gaily striped curtains of heavy silk. There were bright rugs of finest silk spread upon the mosaic floors and divans piled high with gorgeous cushions.

Soon two more servants appeared carrying little pearl-inlaid tables. Two others followed carrying brass trays of little sweet cakes, and great platters of oranges, peaches, and grapes, dates, figs, and pomegranates. Other servants followed bearing upon their heads great deep jars.

When the children had eaten and drunk as much as they—even Sandy—required, Ali Suleiman leaned forward and very softly said, 'Now indeed you must tell me about yourselves. Your parents, are they with you?'

The children shook their heads.

'An aunt? An uncle? A grown-up friend perhaps?'

Again they shook their heads.

'When did you leave England?' Prince Ali inquired.

'Twelve o'clock this morning,' said Humphrey.

'Impossible!' And the prince spread out his hands. 'I offer you my friendship. I give you my hospitality, and I do not find it agreeable that you should tell me lies.'

Peter flushed deeply.

'We would not dream of telling you lies, sir, and we are grateful for all your kindness to us, really we are, but if we told you all the truth you wouldn't believe it.'

'So, you admit that you deceived me! And why should I not believe all the truth?' inquired the prince smoothly.

'Because you couldn't. No grown-up could,' said Peter.

'Even if you saw for yourself you'd think you were dreaming,' added Sheila.

'See what?' asked the prince sharply.

'I think we ought to tell him,' cried Sandy.

'I agree,' said the prince gently.

Peter looked troubled. Then he said, 'Will you excuse me, sir, while I talk to the others for a moment?'

The prince bowed.

'I mean in private,' Peter explained blushing again.

Once more the prince bowed and then walked to the other end of the room.

'I think we'll have to tell him the truth,' said Peter.

'He won't believe it if we do!' Sheila objected.

Humphrey said slowly, 'If he didn't believe us, it would be all right! But if he *did* believe us—'

'You don't think he'd *steal* it!' cried Sandy indignantly. 'Why, he's a prince!'

'A lot of difference that would make!' Peter said grimly. 'Look here, I'm afraid we'll have to tell him *something* because he's getting wild, and I'm sure he won't be a nice customer to deal with then, in spite of what Sandy thinks!'

'You're just being silly!' cried Sandy.

'I hope I am!' said Peter still grimly. He went over to Ali Suleiman Ferouz.

'We *did* come in a flying-ship,' he said, 'but not in an airship. I mean not an ordinary one. It was a *magic* ship.'

'A magic ship!' The prince burst into jolly laughter. But Peter, looking at him closely, thought that perhaps he didn't look as jolly as he sounded.

'The sun must have affected your heads, children,' he said kindly.

Peter said politely, 'Thank you very very much for all your kindness to us, I think we ought to be going now.'

'No!' said the prince still gently. 'I could not dream of allowing four children affected by the sun to go out into the streets alone.'

Peter felt anger rise in his heart. But more than anger, he felt fear.

'We're perfectly all right, thank you,' he said even more politely than before, 'and we really must go.'

'Must?' repeated the prince. '*Must!* It is a long time since any one was so bold as to use that word to Prince Ali Suleiman Ferouz, and what happened to that man was not pleasant. But that need not concern us since we are friends,

are we not? Either you are all sick with the heat of the sun
that you babble of magic ships and must therefore rest in a
dark place until you are well, or you make a mock of me, and
that I will not allow!'

'We are not ill, sir,' Peter said, hoping that his voice did
not show how frightened he was. 'And as for making fun of
you, we wouldn't do that, really we wouldn't.'

The prince's mouth closed like a trap. He looked anything
but kind now.

'If you are neither sick, nor joking,' he said, 'you will show
me this magic ship of which you speak.'

Peter shook his head. 'I'm sorry, sir,' he said politely.

'I give you five minutes in which to consider,' said Ali
Suleiman Ferouz. He turned his back and walked again to
the other end of the room.

'Can't we cut and run?' suggested Sheila.

Humphrey shook his head. 'We shouldn't know the way.
Besides, he's watching us in that looking-glass,' he
whispered.

'He's all right, really he is,' said Sandy loyally. 'Do let's
show him the ship.'

'Not on your life!' Peter said grimly. 'Thank heavens we
haven't got it with us. He knows well enough we're not upset
by the sun or making fun of him or anything like that. He
believes us all right. Lots of Egyptians believe in magic. He
wants the ship for himself.'

'Of course he does! He thinks we can't see through him!'
agreed Humphrey.

The prince took a gold watch from his pocket.

'Three more minutes,' he said in the pleasant voice that did not match his unpleasant eyes, 'and then the sick children must see my physician; but I regret to say he is not always pleasant, my physician.'

Suddenly Sheila said very softly, 'I've got a plan!'

The others looked at her hopefully.

'It's pretty desperate,' she went on, 'but I think we could pull it off. And anyhow it's our only chance. Listen, and don't say a word till I've finished. We've got to take him to see the ship.'

'*What!*' cried Peter and Humphrey together.

'Do wait till I've finished,' implored Sheila, 'we haven't got much time. Let's offer to show him how the magic works.'

'But we can't take him with us!' Peter objected.

'Well, we've simply *got* to get back to the ship,' Sheila reminded them. 'And we can't be worse off than we are!'

'I suppose it's our only chance,' said Peter not very hopefully.

'But what are we going to do when we get there?' asked Humphrey. 'How on earth can we get rid of him?'

'I don't *know*!' answered Sheila in a worried voice. 'We'll just have to wait and see what turns up. All agree?'

She looked anxiously at one after another. One after another they nodded.

Peter went over to Ali Suleiman Ferouz.

'I'm sorry you don't believe us, sir,' he said; 'if you like we'll show you our magic boat.'

'That would be of the very greatest interest, would it not?'

smiled the prince, showing all his teeth. 'Come, we will go at once.'

The children followed him out of the great silk-hung room. They were not sorry to leave it behind, indeed they were all hoping heartily that they would never see it again. Outside the door in the white wall stood the cream car shimmering in the heat. The white-clad chauffeur sprang to attention.

'It's just outside the city walls,' said Peter, 'a couple of miles from the gate, by that big block of half-buried stone.'

The car sped swiftly along the hot and dusty road. Soon, too soon, the city walls came into view. The car stopped.

The prince stepped out first and took each little girl firmly by the hand; the chauffeur followed hard on the heels of the two boys. There was no chance of escape!

Peter went straight over to the great block of stone and the others followed him. The prince reached out an arm and gripped Peter by the shoulder. It was a grip of steel and it hurt, but Peter gave no sign. He stood still for a moment to measure the distance with his eye, then he went straight to the spot.

As his fingers dug at the soft sand he could feel the prince's eyes following his every movement, the prince's breath stirring his hair. He was thinking desperately, 'Two of them! We'll never be able to get rid of two of them!'

His fingers touched the magic boat. Bending close to it, and pretending to dig still deeper into the sand, he whispered, 'Home! *Please!*'

At last the little boat came into view. The prince took a

quick step forward, but before he could so much as touch it, the boat began to grow. Peter put it down on the ground and stood in front, ready to protect it with his life.

'I'll show you how it works!' he offered.

The two Egyptians stood there with the eyes starting out of their heads, their mouths wide open. At any other time the children would have laughed, it all looked so ridiculous; but at this moment they were too sick with fear to laugh at anything.

As soon as the boat was large enough, the prince stepped inside.

'Fly!' he commanded.

But the boat did not stir. It only went on growing.

'So he did mean to steal it,' Humphrey whispered to Sandy.

'Fly! Fly! Fly!' shouted the prince.

Peter said quietly, 'It's no good, Your Highness. It won't fly till it's the proper size.'

The prince stood there scowling blackly.

When the ship was large enough the four children stepped on board.

The boat stopped growing.

The chauffeur made a movement forward. 'No room!' cried Peter, pushing him aside as the boat rose into the air.

The prince laughed heartily at the sight of his grave chauffeur sprawling head over heels in the dust. Then he turned to Peter. 'Oh, you shall be punished for this,' he said, and he was still smiling. 'Oh, how you shall be punished!' He stood staring over the gunwale, lost in wonder as the city walls slipped backwards.

Sheila cast one look at his back, then she lifted her hands and began to spell out their own code. Her heart was beating so loudly that she wondered why Ferouz did not turn at the sound. Could she be quick enough to finish before he turned? And if she went too fast, would the others understand? Her quick fingers flicked through the air. Humphrey and Peter watched her, absorbed and fascinated.

Her fingers dropped to her lap as Ferouz turned suddenly round. But her heart was singing. The message had been given and understood.

Now the ship was flying low over the level fields of brightest green, now it had left the plain far behind and was skimming over bare rock standing out golden against the sapphire sky. But always there went with them the green waters of the Nile.

'Look!' shrieked Sheila suddenly. The prince bent over and the four children together gave him one tremendous push. The spray of the water leaped from the Nile as he fell, and brushed the sides of the low-flying ship. The ship made a sudden leap into the air.

'Good-bye, good-bye, good-bye!' cried the children, laughing as his scarlet fez bobbed wildly on the green water.

'He won't break his neck,' said Peter sadly.

'But there might be crocodiles,' was Humphrey's hopeful suggestion.

'Let's hope so!' exclaimed Sheila and Sandy together.

'Good-bye, good-bye, good-bye!' cried the children as the magic ship rose still higher in the air and set a steady course for home.

CHAPTER 6
Frey's Ship

The children were down on the beach. School was over and they were free for the long summer holiday. Sheila lay quite flat, a large straw hat shading her eyes. In her drowsy ears was the murmur of the waves. She was three-quarters asleep. Sitting in the shade of the rock, Peter was reading. So absorbed was he that he did not even hear the remarks that Humphrey made to him from time to time. Humphrey was busy modelling the sort of desert island he hoped to be wrecked on one day. It was just the right sort of island to be wrecked on, with pineapples and peaches and rainbow-coloured humming-birds and coral strands—in fact everything that a proper desert island ought to have. Sandy was wandering a little distance away, hopefully searching for diamonds, sapphires, rubies, or whatever precious stones the beach might produce. It is true that no one had found either sapphires or diamonds or rubies on this particular bit of beach, but that, Sandy was convinced, was because they hadn't looked hard enough.

Suddenly Peter gave a long whistle. Sheila and Humphrey jumped in surprise.

'Listen to this!' cried Peter, and his voice was trembling with excitement.

'*It is the best of ships. When her sails are hoisted a breeze springs up and carries her swift and safe to whatever place the gods choose. She is made of thousands of little pieces fitted together with so much cleverness that when she is not wanted Frey can fold her up and put her in his pocket.*'

'Well, what do you think of that?' he asked.

'Our ship!' cried Humphrey looking as though he could hardly believe his ears.

'What is?' asked Sandy sauntering up with her pockets full of stones.

'It's in a book—Peter's reading it,' Humphrey explained.

Sheila pushed the hat farther over her nose. 'Tell us about it, Pete,' she said.

'Well, it's a book of old stories. About gods and things. Not Zeus and his crowd—a much better lot. Odin and Frigga. And Thor. And—Frey.'

'I know all about them,' Sandy said. 'We're doing them at school.'

'Well,' continued Peter, 'Frey—'

'Had a magic sword,' interrupted Sandy.

Peter said slowly, 'He had something else magic, too. He had a ship. It was made by the dwarfs. Odin gave it to Frey for a wedding present.'

'How on earth did he manage to lose a thing like that!' Sheila wondered.

'Perhaps a giant stole it. Or the dwarfs,' suggested Sandy. 'The land was full of them in those days.'

'Giants and dwarfs!' breathed Humphrey, forgetting all about his desert island. 'I wish we lived in those days!'

'Do you?' cried Sheila suddenly. '*Do* you?' She sat up, her cheeks scarlet with excitement.

'Do you think our boat can take us anywhere?' she asked abruptly.

Peter stared at her in some surprise. 'You know it can!' he said.

'I don't mean just anywhere—like France, or Greece or Egypt or even Timbuctoo wherever that is! I mean back, back into history.'

'Whatever are you talking about?' asked Peter.

'I mean if it's magic,' she was stammering with excitement, 'we could go backwards. Into history. We could see Cromwell and Wolsey—'

'And Horatius and Hannibal,' said Humphrey who didn't admire her taste.

'And Cinderella,' said Sandy.

'And Pharaoh and Moses,' said Peter.

'And everything, just think, *everything*!' added Sandy.

'Adam and Eve—' Sheila began.

'And pinch me!' finished Sandy.

Humphrey leaned forward and gave her a sharp little nip. She gave a little howl and then subsided.

'Let's try!' urged Sheila.

'But we don't know what might happen,' replied Peter.

'It would be an adventure,' added Humphrey.

Peter looked thoughtful. 'It *would* be an adventure,' he agreed slowly, 'only it might be an awfully dangerous one. On the other hand, nothing might happen, nothing at all. Still, if you all want to—'

'Rather!' interrupted Humphrey.

Still rubbing the pinched spot, Sandy nodded. 'After all, we can come back the minute we don't like it,' she said, 'we've got the boat!'

Peter took the ship out of his pocket.

'To the home of the Norse gods,' he cried. 'To Asgard!'

The ship began to grow immediately. The bright silken sails unfurled and began to swell, although there was no sign of wind.

'It *is*, it's Frey's ship!' cried Peter. 'Look at the sails! It says "*When its sails are hoisted a breeze springs up . . .*"'

'Gosh!' said Humphrey.

As soon as the children stepped inside, the ship rose high into the air. Suddenly it stopped dead. A great black cloud was racing swiftly over the sky. It enfolded the magic boat and the four children shivered in the cold and the darkness.

'What's happened?' Sandy asked anxiously.

'I don't know!' Sheila whispered back, and patted her little sister's hand.

'No need to *whisper*,' Peter said in what he hoped was an everyday sort of voice, though he couldn't help remembering that the ship had never stopped short before.

'But then we've never gone back into history before,' said Humphrey, who knew quite well what Peter was thinking because he'd been thinking that way himself.

For what seemed ages the children sat perfectly still, staring into the solid blackness. It was darker than the darkest tunnel, and they could not see even each others' faintest outline.

'Look!' cried Humphrey suddenly. 'I believe it's getting lighter.'

The four children peered anxiously through the chilly darkness.

'Is it?' asked Sheila. 'Is it?' she stared again into the darkness that covered them. 'Yes,' she said at last, 'I believe it is!'

'It *is*!' Peter said quietly.

They remained sitting very still in their places. Gradually the darkness began to thin at the edges. A faint grey broke through.

'It's like the dawn,' whispered Sheila.

'Look, the sun's coming through,' said Humphrey.

The grey sky was stained with rose as at sunset. The light deepened in broad bands. Suddenly the sun burst through, fierce and bright as after a storm. The sky was clear and very blue about them. Then so slowly, that at first the children did not know it was happening, the ship began to move. It gathered speed and was soon once more cleaving its way like a strong-winged bird.

The children stared at each others' pale faces.

'That *was* a scare!' Peter confessed.

'I'd hate to be lost up in the sky,' Humphrey admitted.

'Perhaps the angels would come and show us the way,' suggested Sandy hopefully.

Now the boat began to sink. When it had grounded, the children stepped out and waited for it to shrink again. Then they looked about them.

The air blew fresh and cool as air on the mountains, the grass was bright, and the sky very blue above them.

'Welcome to my city of Asgard,' said a deep voice behind them.

The children swung round in surprise at these unexpected words.

Before them stood an old man, very tall and upright, carrying his staff as though it were a king's sceptre. There was something so noble about the old man that the children knew, in spite of his simple tunic and broad-brimmed hat, that he must be a king at the very least.

Peter was looking in a puzzled way at the newcomer. He was sure that he had seen him before, quite, quite sure. But where, he had not the slightest idea.

Suddenly his heart gave a leap. This old man with the kingly bearing wore a patch covering one eye. A patch! thought Peter. Now where had he seen an old man wearing a patch, just such a patch before?

His mind went back to the dark old shop that he had never been able to find again, and the bent old man who had sold him the magic ship. One so noble and royal, and the other so bent and poor—was there, *could* there be any connexion between them?

The old man must have read his thoughts, for he smiled very kindly, and, dropping his hand upon Peter's shoulder, said, 'This thing is beyond your understanding, my child. Think no further on the matter and maybe you will read the riddle in the end. Who knows? Meanwhile the air is fresh and the day golden and my palace is near at hand. The young should enjoy themselves while they may, so come!'

It was curious how they followed with no thought of

71

disobeying, or arguing even. He spoke and they obeyed. They followed the lordly stranger over the bright grass, brighter than any they had ever seen before. Soon they saw in the distance the great white walls of a city blinding in the sunshine.

'This is my city,' said the old man, 'and it is called Asgard.'

The great golden gates stood open and the old man and the children passed through.

It was so fair a sight that greeted them that they stood open-mouthed at the great towers and springing fountains, and the bright-coloured flowers, many of which they had never seen before. Everything was as bright and fresh as if it had been new-made that minute.

Out of a great palace doorway stepped a woman. She was the fairest woman the children had ever seen. Her eyes were as blue as the flax flower, and her long hair fell in two braids of new-minted gold, and was intertwined with jewels. She wore a long blue robe with wide sleeves, and on her head was a crown of gold. But even without the crown the children would have known she was a queen, by her beauty and her kindliness and her courtesy.

She held out both hands to greet them.

'My name is Frigga,' she said. 'Welcome to Asgard.'

She took each little girl by the hand, and the others followed through the great white doorway.

'The name of my palace,' said Frigga, 'is *Gladsheim.*'

'It looks a glad sort of place,' observed Humphrey.

On a golden stool lay a distaff with a mist of blue and white thread swirling about it like a cloud. Frigga laughed as she saw the children's eyes rest upon it. 'Yes,' she said, reading their thoughts, 'it *is* cloud. I spin the clouds into the finest linen for the gods to wear. I am the mother of the gods and I am called *The Spinner of the Clouds.*'

'Have you many children, ma'am?' asked Sheila, remembering that queens were always called *ma'am.*

'Yes, a great many,' answered Frigga, smiling.

'Can we play with them?' asked Sandy.

'I think you would find them too old, and some of them, maybe, too rough!' said Frigga, smiling more than ever. 'My children are grown men and women.'

'Goodness!' cried Sheila, and went scarlet.

'Come, tell me your thoughts,' said Frigga, and she smiled.

'Nothing!' said Sheila, and she blushed more than ever.

'Come, now!' said Frigga, and she laughed outright.

'Well,' stammered Sheila, 'I thought—I mean—you see—well, you don't look like the mother of lots and lots of grown-up people.'

'I am older than the stars,' said Frigga.

'You don't look it,' said Sandy.

'How old do the stars look?' asked Frigga, laughing again.

Peter turned suddenly to Odin who had been standing silent, listening to the conversation with a kindly smile upon his face.

'Is the hall of heroes here, in Gladsheim?' he asked.

'Valhalla? Yes, it is the great hall of this house.'

'And the best heroes in the world come here?' asked Peter.

Odin nodded. 'Those that die in battle. It is their reward!'

'They must look grand in their armour. I bet it shines like anything!'

'The armour is dinted and stained as becomes a warrior,' replied Odin.

'How I should love to see them!' cried Humphrey.

'You *shall* see them!' promised Odin.

The children looked at each other with shining faces.

Odin smiled. 'You shall sup with me in The Hall of Heroes. No child before your time has ever supped with Odin in Valhalla, nor shall any child that is to come!'

For a moment the children were silent, it was so great a moment for them that they could not speak. At last Sandy found her voice.

'Who is the bravest warrior?' she asked.

'They are all so brave that no man can say. But the greatest of them all is my son, Thor. Thor wages unceasing fight against the giants, and will do so to the end of time.'

'There aren't any giants where we live,' said Humphrey sadly. 'Except at fairs and things, and they aren't real giants at all.'

'There are always giants,' replied Odin, 'and men must always fight against them.'

'I don't know what you mean,' said Sandy, lifting a puzzled face.

'I understand,' said Sheila softly, 'you mean fighting against things that are wrong.'

Odin nodded. 'Even children may fight that fight,' he said. 'Come!'

They followed Odin through a noble corridor and then

into the largest hall, they, or any one else in the whole world
had ever seen. It stretched so far away that they could not see
the end of it. The great wooden and gold-inlaid walls were
pierced by high and mighty doors.

'There are five hundred and forty,' said Odin, noticing
how the children's glances strayed curiously.

'Why so many?' asked Sheila.

'For all the warriors,' explained Odin. 'They are so
numerous that no man may count them.'

Soon, with a mighty clash of arms, the warriors trooped in.
The noise of crashing steel, of great laughter and full deep
voices filled the mighty hall. Odin, followed by the four
children, went to the head of the enormous table. The end of
the table they could not see, for it stretched far away into the
greatness of the hall. Odin sat down with Peter and Sheila on
one hand, and Humphrey and Sandy on the other. Fair
warrior-maidens, their golden tresses streaming over the
bright armour of their breast-plates, carried round great
pitchers of foaming mead. Odin carved the great boar that
smoked in front of him. He went on carving but the boar
never grew less. A maiden carried to each man his portion.
They fell to with great appetite, for to each man the food
tasted of what he liked best.

Now the great hall was full of the sound of merry feasting,
of the cries of warriors calling aloud for more meat, and the
light footfalls of maidens carrying food and wine. At last, the
feasting was over, and Odin was about to call for his
minstrel, when a cunning-looking, red-haired god rose and
cried:

'A boon, Father Odin!'

'What is your boon, Loki?' asked Odin coldly.

'Let these strangers tell us whence they are come, and why they have come, and how!'

Odin looked troubled and was about to refuse, when there came a great clash of drinking-horns upon the table and the heroes and gods cried with one voice, 'Aye! Aye!'

Odin, still troubled, looked at Peter, then he nodded unwillingly. Peter stood up in his place. He looked very small, standing there, facing that mighty company.

'We came from England,' he said. 'We flew in my ship. We thought of coming here because I was reading in a book about a magic ship like mine.'

A golden chair went spinning backwards and a handsome youth stood up, his eyes sparkling, his cheeks scarlet with excitement. His angry head tossed the gold hair backwards.

'What is this magic ship, Father Odin?' he demanded.

Odin turned to Peter. 'You must tell Frey,' he said.

'It's a ship that flies through the air,' Peter explained, 'and when you have finished with it, it folds up so small you can put it in your pocket.'

'Has it a boar's head of gold upon the prow?' demanded the youth.

Peter nodded.

'My ship! At last my ship!' cried Frey. He strode round the great table and stood in front of Peter, holding out his hand.

Peter's hand went into his pocket and stayed there as if to protect his beloved little ship.

'My ship!' cried Frey, his eyes glittering with anger. 'Give me my ship! '

Odin stood up in his place and silence fell.

'Son Frey,' he exclaimed, 'this is no manner in which to treat a guest of Odin, nor is this any time for brawling. Come now, calm yourself, and then I will judge.'

Frey went back to his place. But he sat there, his eyes still glowing with fury.

Then, still standing in his place, Odin cried, 'To the Peace Stead, for this thing must be settled in friendship.'

Then with a great noise of clinking steel, the gods and warriors followed Odin and his guests from Valhalla. Soon they reached the green and peaceful meadow of the Peace Stead, where no man may raise his voice in anger, and where no slightest shadow of quarrelling may come. Odin and Frigga seated themselves upon their high thrones of gold. On the right-hand stood Peter, tightly clutching his boat. On the left, stood Frey, his hand upon his empty sword-belt.

All around stood the mighty throng, gods and goddesses bright and proud in the sunset—and Red Loki the mischief-maker, smiling in his beard at the trouble he had brought forth. Behind them stood the vast array of heroes, their dinted armour flashing in the red evening light.

A little to one side, very small and lonely, stood the three other children, looking anxious, and wondering what would happen to them if Frey were to gain possession of the magic ship. Would they ever get home again?

When all was silent, Odin spoke.

'Frey,' he said, 'speak you first.'

Frey took a step forward. 'It is my ship, my own ship, as indeed you know, for it was you yourself that gave it me as a gift when I was wedded to Gerda the Fair.'

Odin nodded. 'But you lost it, Frey!' he said.

'It was stolen from me!'

'Were you sleeping, Frey, that you allowed so priceless a possession to be stolen?' asked Odin.

'It was stolen by enchantment!' cried Frey fiercely. 'Carried across the sea to Jotunheim, home of the giants, for all I know. And how *should* I know, seeing that I must never leave Asgard and my work of watching over all growing things? Frey must not seek his own, lest famine fall upon Asgard and the world of men starve.'

'This is idle talk,' replied Odin. 'You lost your ship as you lost your magic sword—because you valued neither at their true worth.'

Frey flushed. 'My sword I gave that I might win in exchange the fairest Gerda, and with that bargain I am well content. But my ship—my ship was stolen.'

He took a stride towards Peter. 'Boy,' he thundered, 'give me back my ship!'

Odin said still gently, 'Peace, Frey, I will have no brawling in the Peace Stead.' He turned to Peter. 'Did you steal this ship?' he asked.

Peter went scarlet and his eyes were as angry as Frey's. For a moment he lost his awe of Father Odin.

'I should jolly well think not!' he cried. 'I bought it!'

Loki let out a great and bitter laugh.

'Where did this child find so great a sum to purchase the ship Skidbladnir? There is no treasure in the whole world can buy it.'

'Answer him, my child,' commanded Odin.

Peter spoke as if in a dream. 'I gave all the money I had in the world—and a bit over!' he answered.

Odin said, 'Frey, it is very clear that Skidbladnir has passed out of your hands. It was yours and you lost it. Now it has come to this child by right of purchase, and it is his until such time as he, of his own free will, shall give it up!'

Frey strode over to Peter. 'What will you take in exchange?' he cried.

Peter looked at Frey. 'If I give up the ship, would you take us home again?'

For a moment Frey did not answer. Then he shook his bright head. 'He who owns the ship may travel where he will—but not into the future, that alone is forbidden. Were the ship mine I could not take you home again.'

'Then I have to keep it,' Peter said simply. 'You see we must get home!'

Odin was thoughtful for a moment, then he lifted his head and spoke.

'Frey,' he said, 'men come and go. The years pass with them more swiftly than the flight of an arrow. But with the gods it is not so. Ages pass, the sea may grow dry and the mountains crumble, but our hair is not less bright, nor our strength less, nor our wits more dim. The gods endure. Now let us strike a bargain. This child shall keep your ship until such time as he no longer desires it, then he shall return it to you!'

A peal of mocking laughter broke in upon the quiet of the Peace Stead. 'Until he no longer desires it!' cried Loki. 'What man is born who would not desire Skidbladnir?'

79

'Silence, mischief-maker!' thundered Odin. 'Shall I sew up your mouth as once before?' Then turning to Frey he said gently, 'There is no magic when one no longer believes. See, son Frey, in a few short years these children will no longer believe in a magic ship. They think now, maybe, that this time will not come, but as surely as the sun rises and sets, come it must. For they will grow to full manhood—and every man must go about his business. Believe me, Frey, the time must come for them not to believe, nor even to remember any more. When that time comes let them give back Skidbladnir, and I will give each in return a gift. How say you, friend Peter?'

'I don't think I understand,' said Peter.

'I understand,' said Sheila slowly. 'You mean when we're grown-up and don't believe any more.'

Odin nodded.

'We'll forget,' Sheila went on sadly. 'Being grown-up does that to you.'

For a moment the four children stood sorrowful and silent, then Peter spoke in a clear voice so that all could hear.

'It shall be as you say, Father Odin. One of these days we shall send back the ship.'

Father Odin laughed. 'Then is this thing well settled. And on the day you send back Skidbladnir, I will grant each one his heart's desire.'

Frey strode forward and clasped Peter by the hand.

'Thanks, brother,' he said, 'guard my ship well. And now I will tell you a secret concerning Skidbladnir that no soul knows, save Father Odin and me. When you alight from the

ship and set foot in a foreign land whose tongue you can
neither speak nor understand, pass each one of you a hand
over the boar's head and the secret of the foreign speech shall
be made clear. And, more, you shall look like the dwellers in
that land and no man shall know you as strangers. And so,
brother, farewell!'

The light streaming from his golden hair seemed to dazzle
the children and almost to blind them. When they could see
clearly again, the sun had dropped and it was full evening.
Asgard and its bright inhabitants had disappeared and the
four of them stood alone on a high dark mountain. The
evening air blew chill upon them and they shivered a little.
Peter drew the ship from his pocket and set it down upon the
stony mountain-side.

'Home!' he commanded.

As the sails of Skidbladnir lifted in the air, they heard a
voice on the wind behind them calling, 'I will grant each one
his heart's desire!'

CHAPTER 7
Matilda

The children were once more down on the beach. They had brought their tea down with them; it was a very good tea, and they were busy enjoying it. Since their journey to Asgard they had been satisfied to play more or less quietly on the beach, for the weather had been very hot and nothing pleased them so much as bathing. And as Humphrey said, 'The sea here is as good as the sea anywhere!' Which was perfectly true. But now a cool wind had sprung up, and since the children had been in the water at least three times that day, Peter asked, 'Who's ready for another adventure?'

Sandy bit into a large fresh doughnut. 'I don't want to be anywhere but here!' she said.

'Little pig!' laughed Sheila.

'She'll change her mind the minute she's finished eating,' said Humphrey.

'We ought to be careful what adventure we choose,' Sheila remarked thoughtfully. 'We nearly got into hot water twice, once with old Ferouz, and once with Frey.'

'Frey was fine,' Peter said dreamily, remembering how the god had taken him by the hand and called him *brother*.

'Still, if it hadn't been for Father Odin we *should* have got into trouble,' added Humphrey.

'That Loki-beast was out for mischief,' said Peter.

'I suppose,' Humphrey said thoughtfully, 'you can't help troubles popping up now and then, even when you don't expect them. I mean, even if we stayed here on this spot without moving, something would happen!'

'I bet it would!' Peter roared with laughter. 'The tide would, you chump!'

'Of course,' Humphrey agreed; 'that's what I meant.'

Sheila broke in quickly to avoid the argument that seemed to be coming. 'Where shall we go?' she asked.

'I think we ought to take it in turn to choose. Sandy chose first, and then Peter did,' said Humphrey. 'Your turn now, Sheila, and next time it will be me.'

Sheila peeled her banana with care. 'Let me see,' she said. Very thoughtfully she bit off the top.

'I'd like to go back to William the Conqueror,' she said at last.

'Whatever for?' asked Sandy, wrinkling up her nose.

'It sounds exciting. I've just been reading about it!' Sheila held up a copy of *Hereward the Wake*.

'William the Conqueror was a beast, wasn't he?' asked Sandy.

'Not always,' replied Sheila. 'I expect you have to be a bit of a bully when you've got to keep thousands and thousands of people in order—especially when they don't want to be kept—'

'Well, why should they be?' Sandy broke in. 'It was their own country!'

Sheila went on as if she hadn't heard.

'He was a good king, really,' she said. 'He made lots and lots of good laws. And he gave the people of London a charter—'

'What's a charter?' asked Sandy.

'A sort of roll of parchment,' Sheila explained. 'And in this charter he promised that no man should do them any wrong.'

'Did he keep his promise?' asked Sandy with great interest.

'Let's hope so,' Sheila replied.

'You've got a hope!' Peter joined in the conversation. 'If you want to know, he burnt all the north where the people wouldn't have him, and he burnt down the villages in the south, and turned the people out of their homes to make a forest to hunt in.'

'The New Forest,' Sheila said dreamily, 'near Bournemouth, where we went last summer. Well, he made a *lovely* forest of it, anyway—'

'Perhaps you wouldn't think it so lovely if *your* house had been burnt down!' Humphrey interrupted.

Sheila took no notice. 'He built churches all over the country—'

'I'm not so keen on churches,' said Sandy, 'you have to sit still all the time.'

'And castles,' Sheila went on, 'great big castles—'

'Castles!' cried Sandy. 'Let's go at once.'

'Full of dungeons, you bet!' said Humphrey. 'I'm not so sure,' he went on slowly, 'that it would be such a good adventure. If the country was full of soldiers because of people rebelling, and if towns and farms and fields were being burnt to punish them for it, well, it sounds to me as though we'd find trouble without looking very far for it!'

'We'd always have the magic ship to bring us back,' Sandy reminded him.

The others nodded.

'Well, if you all want to go,' Humphrey said, 'let's go!'

They bundled the plates and cups and saucers and flasks into the tea-basket, and they were particularly careful to see that there were no paper-bags lying about, then they pushed the basket into the shelter of the rocky cove.

'Goodness!' cried Peter suddenly, and he stood stock-still, with his eyes very bright.

'What's the matter?' asked Sheila.

'I've just thought of something,' said Peter in a very excited voice. 'We'll have to do what Frey said. You know, pass our hand over the boar's head so that we'll look just like everybody else.'

'I wonder what it'll feel like, being different,' said Humphrey in a wondering voice.

'We'll see soon enough,' Sandy remarked.

'What are we going to be?' asked Sheila. 'Norman or English?'

'English of course!' said Humphrey at once.

'It won't be so pleasant being English with all those Norman soldiers about,' Sandy said. 'I expect they'll have swords and bows and arrows and everything!'

'I expect they will,' said Humphrey firmly. 'All the same I'm going to be English.'

'So am I!' agreed Peter.

'Me, too!' added Sheila.

'All right,' said Sandy. 'And if we get into a tight corner don't blame me!'

'What language do you suppose we'll speak?' asked Peter.

'English to the English and Norman to the Normans,' replied Humphrey.

'What on earth shall we look like?' Sandy wondered.

'I've got a picture in my book,' Sheila said.

Three eager heads bent over the page while Sheila pointed out the picture of a boy in a short tunic with long tight sleeves, his legs bound about with bands of cloth.

'Gosh!' said Humphrey. 'I hope there's a pair of trousers underneath, I'd feel dreadful without trousers.'

'I think it's awfully nice,' exclaimed Sandy. 'Now let's look at the girls.'

She looked at the picture of the long gown sweeping to the floor and the long, wide sleeves. 'Do you mean to say *children* were dressed like that—children like us?' she asked in surprise.

Sheila nodded.

'Well I'm jolly glad I didn't live then,' Sandy said. 'I shouldn't think that sort of dress would be very handy for playing in.'

'No,' agreed Peter, looking over her shoulder, 'you wouldn't have much fun in a thing like that!'

'Awkward sort of dress if you had to get away in a hurry,' Humphrey said thoughtfully.

'Why on earth *should* we want to get away in hurry?' asked Peter.

'Well, you never know! We did once. And we nearly did twice!'

'Humphrey's right,' Sheila said firmly. 'We'd better all dress as boys, boys' things will be easier to run away in.'

'Hooray!' cried Sandy, dancing on one foot. 'I'd *like* to be a boy!'

'Then that's settled!' said Sheila. 'Every one ready?'

Unable to speak for excitement, the others nodded. Peter took his ship out of his pocket and placed it on the sand. 'Take us to Norman England!' he commanded.

The boat rose with the children high into the air. Then it stopped short. The black cloud came racing along the sky and in a moment had enveloped them. But this time they were not afraid. Soon the cloud thinned and the boat remained perched motionless in the clear sky.

'It isn't moving,' cried Humphrey in surprise.

'Give it a chance!' replied Peter who could not believe that his beloved ship would ever fail them.

'It's dropping again,' cried Sheila anxiously. 'Look it's going down straight as a stone. We shall land where we started from.'

Sure enough the boat was dropping in a straight line and in a moment it had grounded on their own familiar beach. On the left the path with the sea-poppies went up towards the road, on the right was the cliff and the cove which they had left a few minutes ago.

The children scrambled out sadly.

'It didn't work at all,' Humphrey said in a sorrowful voice. 'Well, I suppose there are limits to what even a magic boat can do!'

Peter made no reply. He was stroking the boar's head gently as if trying to assure it that he was not in the least disappointed.

'Well,' exclaimed Sheila in what she hoped was a bright and cheerful voice. 'There's our own cove. Let's collect the basket and take it back to the house.'

Sandy ran towards the cove and then came running back to join the others. She was waving her arms about, and it looked as though she were trying to tell them something.

'It's gone!' she cried when at last she could make herself understood.

'What's gone?' asked Sheila, running to meet her.

'The basket!' cried Sandy.

'I bet you didn't look properly,' said Humphrey.

'I bet I did!'

'Of course it's there!' said Peter. 'Why it's only a minute or two since we left it!'

'All right!' said Sandy. 'If you don't believe me, come and see for yourselves!'

The four children raced over the sand towards the cove.

It was quite true. There was no sign of the basket.

'Perhaps some one's hidden it for a lark,' suggested Peter.

'No one ever comes here. Besides, there's no sign of footsteps except those we've just made,' said Humphrey.

Peter whistled thoughtfully. 'That's odd,' he said. 'Where are our footsteps? I mean the ones we made when we came down to the cove first?'

'It *is* queer,' Sheila agreed, wrinkling her brows.

'I wonder what could have happened!' said Humphrey thoughtfully.

Very puzzled they walked slowly up the well-known gap-path towards home. Peter gave another long whistle.

'It's gone!' he cried.

'What's gone?' asked the three others together.

Peter waved in the direction of the house.

He was right. The house was gone. The street and the road and the red motor-buses were gone too.

'It's like you take a rubber and rub things out,' said Sandy.

'It must be the sun,' said Sheila faintly.

Suddenly Humphrey gave a loud cry. 'It isn't the sun,' he exclaimed. 'It's all right. Everything's all right. We're back!'

'I know we're back!' Peter said bitterly.

'I don't mean that! I mean back—back in history. You said Norman England, didn't you? Well, Norman England is any bit of England, isn't it? There isn't any reason why it shouldn't be our own bit, is there?'

'He's right,' Sheila said slowly. 'After all, the sea and the cliffs and the beach might well look the same, mightn't they?'

'And that's why the basket's gone. It's lying on the beach in 1939.'

'Our adventure's happened. It's happened!' cried Sandy, dancing for joy.

'Quick, the boat!' cried Humphrey.

'Whatever for?' asked Sheila. And then suddenly she understood. 'Of course,' she cried. 'We've got to look like every one else! Quick!'

Peter drew his boat from his pocket and set it in the middle of the empty sandy path. Then he passed his hand over the head of the boar. Humphrey followed his example. As Sheila passed her hand over the golden boar, she whispered, 'Sandy and I would like to be dressed as boys!'

Then they stood staring at each other.

'It's worked!' said Sheila at last in a funny little voice.

'Of course it has!' exclaimed Peter as if he had never doubted the power of his magic ship.

'You look exactly like the boy in Sheila's book!' cried Humphrey breathlessly.

'So do you! We all do!' cried Sandy, and went head over heels in sheer delight.

'Don't let's waste any more time,' said Peter, and they went on up the cliff path.

'Looks like a village or something down there,' cried Humphrey, pointing to a blue haze rising from the sky. 'And o-o-oh, there's a castle or something over there, look!'

The others looked in the direction of his pointing finger. A cluster of wooden huts, from which the blue smoke curled lazily, lay about the feet of a four-square tower. A bright pennon stirred gently in the wind.

The four children set off in the direction of the castle.

As they neared the thatched and wooden cottages, a dog rushed out barking and snapping.

'Down!' cried Peter, and the four children stared at each other. The word was new on his lips, and yet they understood—for the language was no longer strange to their ears.

A woman came out of a low hut and stood blinking angrily in the evening sunlight.

'Who are you, and whence do you come? You are of

churlish manners,' she went on without waiting for an answer. 'You should know well enough that no man may enter a village that is not his own, without first sounding the great horn.'

'What great horn? And why?' asked Sandy.

The woman held up her hands in astonishment. 'What children are you,' she asked, 'that do not know our custom? If you do not sound the great horn how shall we know whether you be friend or foe?'

Peter said, 'You know well that we are no evil-doers. And as for the old custom, it is put by, since William became our lord and king.'

'Nay, I know nothing. The old customs were good customs. And the old days were good days. And what is more, these are bad times. One day you live in peace in the house you have built for yourself, and the next, who knows, but the house is burnt about your head, and you wander forth, starving.'

Sandy thought that the woman with her red fat face looked very far from starving, but she kept her thoughts to herself.

'Besides,' the woman was going on angrily, 'by the looks of you, you should be good Saxon—you have the right Saxon look, except maybe the lad there—' and she nodded at Peter. 'He looks to be of kin to the high-nosed Normans. Are you not ashamed to prate of William your lord? Have you forgotten Harold your king that died for you on Senlac field? And Edgar the Aetheling, who is your rightful lord?'

A great hand clapped itself over her mouth. A sturdy man, his cheeks pale with fear, stood behind her.

'Hold your tongue, woman!' he ordered. 'Do you want our house to burn about our ears for this talk? You must know, gentles,' he went on, addressing the children, 'my wife is of small wit. William of Normandy is our king, and to him and to none other do we owe allegiance. As for the silly quacking of the woman here, I pray you, forget it, every word.'

Peter's chin went up. 'We know how to hold our tongues,' he said.

'The Lord be praised!' cried the man with all his heart. 'It is rare, indeed, to find children of such wisdom. These days no man knows who may be his friend, nor who his enemy. But now it grows late, and we must go to our beds. My harvest fields are ready, and before I may bring in my own grain, I must give service at the castle to bring in the lord's wheat, so I must rise betimes. Give you good night, gentles!'

The children stood gaping as the wooden door of the cottage swung to and shut firmly in their faces. They could hear the heavy bar being let down on the latch, and then the drawing of the bolts.

'But it's early yet,' cried Sandy in surprise. 'Not more than seven, I should say! Surely they won't go off to bed now!'

'Country people always went to bed early—now—I mean those days,' said Humphrey.

'Save the candles!' Sheila explained. 'When you have to make your own, you think twice before you use them dashingly.'

The great drawbridge of the castle was down. The birds flew overhead, their wings black against the rosy sky. It was all very quiet and very peaceful.

Their backs turned to the children, two soldiers gossiped, leaning on their pikes.

'How are we going to get by?' whispered Sheila.

Peter said softly, 'Duck, and take your chance!'

They crouched flattened against the wall. A thick bell-rope dangled from the bell-tower. The soldiers were still gossiping with their backs turned to the children. Peter darted from his place. He had given a violent tug at the bell-rope and ducked down breathless before the single sharp note had died away in the quiet air.

At the sound of the bell, the two soldiers straightened themselves, and dashed over the drawbridge. There was no one in sight. They walked down the road, one turning to the left and the other to the right.

'Quick!' cried Peter. Lightly and swiftly the children fled over the drawbridge and into the court-yard. To the left stood a long low wooden shed with its door wide open, and they dodged inside. They could hear the two men returning and grumbling loudly at the trick that had been played upon them.

'It must be that young devil Gurth,' complained one, 'I boxed his ears yesterday.'

'I'll do more than box his *ears*!' growled the other. 'If he sits down for a week after this, he's lucky!'

'Still it was curfew-time, in any case,' the other reminded him. 'Look, the shadow has reached the well-head already. It's your turn!'

The other went over the drawbridge and back to the bell-rope. Soon the quiet air was full of clangour, the quiet court-yard busy with the coming and going of folk about their business. Maids and men thronged over the great cobbled stones. Girls let their pitchers down the well, or came across the court-yard carrying great piles of sweet-smelling linen. Hens and chickens flew squawking as they were chased from underfoot. The drover guided his pigs into the sties. Dogs barked, donkeys brayed, pigs grunted, cocks crowed, men shouted, and maids scolded. The quiet court-yard had become as busy as a fairground on bank holiday.

Crouched in a dark corner of the dark outhouse, the children wondered how in the world they were going to get out, and what would happen to them when they did.

Presently a shadow fell through the half-open door. A voice cried in good Saxon, 'Fasten back the door and then come help me bring in the beasts.'

The sound of doors being dragged back came to their ears, and presently a mooing, and the steady trot of feet, told the children that the cows were coming in for the night.

'I don't *like* cows!' whispered Sandy.

'Sh!' Peter whispered back, 'they won't hurt you. They're as tame as tame. Keep quiet and don't fuss, and we'll get out of this soon enough.'

The quiet creatures came swaying in from the red sunlit court-yard into the darkness of the byre. Sheila put out a hand and stroked the first-comer. Sandy, too, stretched out a timid hand. The gentle creature let out a friendly moo. Soon there was no sound in the shed but the occasional lowing of a cow anxious to be milked, and the steady rattle of milk as it dropped into the pail. The men went backwards and forwards carrying the foaming buckets.

'I'm thirsty!' whispered Sandy.

'Sh!' warned Peter.

In and out went the men, and soon the last of the milk had been carried out.

'We must get away before they come back to bolt up,' whispered Humphrey, 'we don't want to stop here all night.'

'Now!' said Peter.

They crept from the shadow of the byre and into the court-yard.

The court-yard was black with people going about their business, and the children mingled unnoticed with the crowd. Soon they came to the great open door of the castle and found themselves outside the large hall. Servants were strewing fresh rushes upon the floor. Some were carrying great baskets of bread, others were putting drinking-horns upon the table.

'Hi there!' cried one, as Peter's head came through the door-way. 'Off to the kitchen, idle fellow, and tell the cook we still lack bread.'

Peter disappeared. He had no intention of finding the kitchen, but a serving-maid, coming up behind, gave him a cuff on the ear. 'Begone about your business, lazy wretch!' she scolded and pushed him before her.

The great ovens and open fires painted the kitchen walls with red light. There was a delicious smell of broiling and stewing. Peter's nose twitched, it was so long since dinner.

One of the cooks, a fat good-natured fellow, turned to Peter with a grin. 'Ho, little starveling,' he laughed, 'your face is new. But I like it well. It puts me in mind of my brother, a little lad, I have left behind me in my own country! When you have finished serving, return again, and I will give you food for yourself.' He thrust into Peter's hand one of the great baskets of bread and the boy went staggering across the court-yard. As he went in at the great door, he saw the others huddled in the darkness.

'Keep down,' he whispered, 'I'll be back in a minute.'

He dumped the basket on a bench in the hall and then ran back to them. Another bell, louder and shriller than the first one, began to ring. Soon there was the noise of many feet tramping across the court-yard.

Hidden in the shadows, the children stood, staring at the procession.

Normans plainly dressed, Normans richly dressed, knights and ladies high-nosed and proud. Humphrey whispered, 'Look!' and stared at a little girl in a long gown of heavy green cloth with wide furred sleeves, and a chain of gold about her neck. The child, who looked about ten years old, carried her small head proudly, looking about her with an air of ill-tempered disdain.

'Horrid little beast,' whispered Sheila.

Humphrey said thoughtfully, 'She'd have quite a nice face if she didn't look so disagreeable.'

The child turned her head as if aware that she was being discussed. Then she lifted her long skirt in one hand, and looking straight in front of her, walked proudly on. A man walked beside her. He was dressed very plainly, his long tunic was dark and of thick woollen material. Yet, though he was dressed a good deal more simply than some, he had the proud air of one used to command. He stood there, looking out of piercing eyes that seemed to miss nothing. The watching children thought that the others shrank before that proud and threatening look. Yet he was pleasant enough with the child, walking with a hand in friendly fashion on her small shoulder, and smiling out of his narrow mouth.

'I bet that's the lord of the castle,' whispered Sandy. 'I don't like his face.'

Neither did the three others. They remained crouched in their corner until the throng had passed into the great hall. In and out bustled the serving-men and women, hurrying backwards and forwards, carrying savoury meats on great platters. The pleasant smell came to the hidden children, making their mouths water.

'I'm *awfully* hungry!' moaned Sandy.

Peter suddenly remembered the cook's promise. 'Wait a bit,' he said, 'I'll get you something.'

'O-o-oh Peter, could you, really?' asked Sandy.

Sheila said quickly, 'Don't, Peter. You might get yourself into trouble. We're not *terribly* hungry!'

Peter stood up. 'That's all right,' he said, and disappeared into the dark court-yard.

The red glare of the kitchen showed him the way. He slipped in through the open door and looked round for the kindly cook. Soon he saw the fat man who sent him a friendly grin. 'It is the little starveling,' he said. 'Here are your meats!' He began to pile a wooden board high with bread and meat. Then he thrust the platter into Peter's hand.

Peter was about to ask for a knife and fork when he saw

that each man was cutting his meat with a knife he took from his girdle. He trembled to think how nearly he had given himself away. His own hand went up to his leather belt, and there, sure enough, hung a knife. As he turned to go, he found the cook looking at him strangely.

'You have the Norman look,' he said, 'so that you put me in mind of my own brother, yet you speak Saxon like a Saxon. What is your name, lad?'

'Peter!'

'Your name is good Norman, yet you say it like a Saxon,' went on the cook, and to himself he thought, 'This is a strange thing! Who has seen this lad before? Not I.'

Peter went out carrying the heaped-up platter of meat and the cook followed him with his eyes.

'Maybe the lad is an enemy,' he thought, 'who will let down the drawbridge, and with his friends burn the castle about our ears while we sleep. My lord must know of it! But not now while he is at meat. As soon as he rises I will go tell him.'

'Hist!' Humphrey's voice came out of the darkness. Peter walked steadily towards him. It was dark now, but he could just make out their shapes as they crouched against the wall.

'I've got the food, but nothing to eat it with,' he grinned.

'Fingers were made before forks,' said Sandy, and sniffed the good smell.

'It's got a queer spicy smell. I hope it won't make us sick,' said Sheila anxiously.

'Gosh, it's *good*!' said Humphrey with his mouth full.

Sandy and Peter said no more. They were far too busy.

They had just finished eating and were wondering what to do next, when the sound of benches scraping, and feet treading, and voices growing louder, told them that the company was rising from its meat.

'Don't move!' came Peter's voice, anxious in the darkness. They remained there crouched against the wall. One or two solitary figures came out from the lighted hall and stood black against the warm light. They saw the governor of the castle step out into the dark court-yard, the little girl clinging to his arm. Then they saw the fat cook dart from the kitchen, cross the length of the court-yard, and stand humbly, his head bent, before his lord. The little girl took her small hand from her father's arm and, lifting her long skirts above the dirt of the cobbles, ran swiftly towards the narrow tower. The door was open and in a moment she was lost to sight.

'Why ever did we have to hide like that?' asked Sheila in a low voice. 'What are you afraid of?'

'I don't know.' Peter was troubled. 'I didn't like the look of the governor-person. I just wanted time to think!'

'If it's as bad as that, let's go home,' suggested Sandy.

'No fear!' Peter was already ashamed of his sudden panic. 'He can't do us any harm—not really. And anyhow, why should he want to try?'

'It's a pity to spoil an adventure in the middle,' Humphrey agreed, 'and we *have* got the ship!'

'I wonder where that door leads to?' said Sheila, looking thoughtfully at the place where the child had disappeared in the darkness.

'Let's go and see,' suggested Peter.

CHAPTER 8

Matilda's Tower; and another Sort of Tower

The tower door swung gently on its hinges and the children pushed it open. They found themselves on a stone spiral staircase; the dark steep stairs went curving away above their heads.

The children began to climb. Up they went. Up and up. It seemed that the stairs curving up into the darkness would go on for ever and ever. At last, tired with climbing, and completely out of breath, they reached the top. A small door stood half-open and the children peeped inside.

It was a small round room high up in the tower. Through the narrow window-slits, the evening air came blowing, stirring the bright woollen curtains that hung against the stone walls. The room was unfurnished, except for a low stool of dark carved wood, a small heavy table heaped with bright-coloured wools, and a low embroidery frame. On the wall a torch flamed, flinging its warm light on stone wall and rush-strewn floor.

'The dear little room,' cried Sheila, 'I wonder who it belongs to?'

Sandy sat down on the stool. The embroidery frame was at arm's level. They could all see that this must be a child's room.

'It belongs to the little girl we saw downstairs,' Humphrey suggested.

'Nasty little thing!' said Sheila.

Suddenly the door flew open and went crashing back against the stone wall. The child herself stood in the doorway, her dark eyes snapping with anger.

'Saxon pigs!' she cried. 'You dare to set foot in my chamber? I will have you whipped. I will have your hands chopped off. I will have your heads taken from your shoulders.'

'Sweet child!' said Peter grinning. 'Is that all?' and now he was laughing so that the tears ran down his face.

She stopped scolding and stared open-mouthed at this new-comer who dared to laugh at the Lady Matilda.

Sandy said sharply, 'Stop being silly! We'll take you away in our magic ship and drop you overboard if you don't behave yourself!'

The child went on staring, speechless with rage. When at last she had recovered her breath, she cried, 'Saxon pigs, yet you speak good Norman! I have never before set eyes on you—nor do I want to, ever again. Who are you?'

Sheila said severely, 'Before we talk to you, you've got to say you're sorry!'

'I won't!' screamed the child and turned her back. 'And what's more,' she swung round again, 'I'm going to tell my father, now, this very minute. He'll throw you into the prison-tower, in chains most likely. I expect the rats will run over your feet. I expect they'll bite your toes. I hope they will, anyhow!'

Sheila was about to retort, but Humphrey said quietly, 'Don't tease her.' He went over to the angry little girl and held out his hand. 'We're friends you know,' he said smiling.

She looked at him for a moment with her fierce eyes, then the anger died out of them. Her two small jewelled hands went out and clasped him by the shoulders. 'Friends!' she said.

'Well that's that!' said Peter, and sat down on the floor. 'Now let's introduce ourselves. This is Sheila and this one's Sandy. That's Humphrey you've just been hugging, and I'm Peter.'

'Why are those girls dressed like boys?' demanded the child.

'I'll explain that in a minute,' Peter promised. 'You tell us your name first.'

'I am Matilda. My father came over with Duke William of Normandy. That was before I was born. My nurse tells me often and often about Normandy. It is a lovely country, she says. And in the spring the apple orchards are in flower and you smell them even when you are asleep. I would like to go back to my own country.'

'Aren't you happy here?' asked Humphrey gently.

Matilda shrugged her thin shoulders. 'My cousins are over there. My mother's sister's children, and my father's sister's also. Here I have no friends.'

'I should think that's your fault,' said Sheila, still severely. She had not forgotten Matilda's display of temper. Matilda's eyes flashed, but she said quietly, 'How should that be? My father is governor of this castle and there is no one but the brats of my father's steward and his clerk. It is not fitting,' she drew herself up to her full height, 'that I should play with them!'

'Then you don't deserve to have any friends!' said Sheila.

'Don't let's quarrel,' Humphrey said. 'Besides she's got friends now, she's got us.'

'Only if she behaves herself,' Sheila added firmly.

'Now,' said Matilda, and her voice was still rather commanding, 'you must tell me where you come from, and why these girls are dressed like boys.'

Peter said, 'It's rather hard to explain. They're dressed like boys because—well, because it's a sort of disguise.'

'Disguise!' Matilda was startled. She knew that disguises nearly always spelt trouble in this rebellious land.

'Well, not really disguised,' Peter explained, 'only it makes the adventure easier.'

'I don't understand,' said Matilda still suspiciously.

'Well, of course it isn't easy,' Humphrey said smiling, 'but we're friends, aren't we? What year is this?' he asked suddenly.

'The year of grace 1073,' said Matilda still looking puzzled.

'Well it's 1939 where we come from,' Peter explained. 'We've come back over eight hundred years to pay you a visit.'

'I don't understand!' said Matilda again.

'Don't try,' said Sandy kindly.

'Just think we're friends who have made a long journey to see you!' advised Peter.

'We'll show you how it's done when we go,' Sheila said more kindly.

'We'll take you back with us, perhaps,' Humphrey said. 'You know we have a magic boat—'

'Witchcraft!' cried Matilda. 'My father would chop off your hands—or your heads, even!' And she shuddered.

'Don't be silly,' Humphrey said affectionately. 'It isn't witchcraft at all. Just plain straightforward magic! We'll show you and then you can see for yourself. Besides, your father won't know anything about us!'

'Unless you tell him!' added Sheila a little sternly.

'I would never tell, never, never!' cried Matilda.

'Let her take the oath!' cried Sandy hopping up and down with excitement.

'No,' said Peter, 'we haven't ever allowed any outsider to share the oath, not even our best friends.'

'Do let her,' Humphrey coaxed, 'then she could be a sort of sister to us!'

'What is this oath?' asked Matilda anxiously.

So Sheila explained. Presently, with fingers tightly crossed, the five children recited the oath.

'Now you are really one of us,' said Sheila.

'It's all very queer,' declared Matilda, looking puzzled but very happy. 'Tell me about yourselves, how you live and what you do!'

'Well there isn't much to tell,' answered Peter. 'We go to school—'

'All of you?' asked Matilda in the greatest surprise.

Peter nodded.

'You are going to be priests or monks, *all* of you?' she asked.

'Oh no!' Humphrey answered in equal surprise. 'What a funny idea!'

'But only priests and monks go to school,' Matilda said.

'I wish I were you!' whispered Sandy.

'Can you read? *All* of you?' asked Matilda.

'Of course!' answered the four of them together.

'And write?' insisted Matilda, her eyes growing rounder and rounder.

'Of course!' Sheila answered a little impatiently.

Matilda shook her head. 'Children that can both read and write,' she exclaimed. 'This is a great marvel!'

'Don't be so silly,' said Sheila and she walked over to the embroidery frame. She looked down at the tapestry. It showed a battle-scene, Normans and Saxons, fighting to the death. The picture was clear and bright, worked in fine wool, with thousands and thousands of tiny regular stitches. So bold was the design that the tiny figures seemed to be moving.

'Whose work is this?' asked Sheila.

Matilda laughed outright. 'But mine, of course. Whose else?'

'But it's beautiful!' Sheila said.

'Oh, that is simple, *simple!*' Matilda assured her. 'Every woman can embroider with her needle. I am not as skilful as many. As for this,' she shrugged her shoulders, 'every one who can lift a needle at all does this tapestry. We copy the queen. Queen Matilda, after whom I am named—she is my

105

godmother—she started this fashion. All the battles in which her lord was victorious she has embroidered in tapestry—the others of course are forgotten. Naturally we must follow the fashion. As for me,' Matilda kicked at the embroidery frame, 'I am weary to death of it!'

'I think it's lovely,' Sheila assured her. 'I wish I were half as clever as you!'

'I am glad you think I am clever,' Matilda said a little wistfully. 'I should love to come with you. It is so dull here. I have no one to talk to, unless it is my nurse—my father sometimes, but not often. You see,' she added softly, 'my mother is dead.'

There was a little silence; the children were so sorry for Matilda that they could not think what to say.

'One day,' the little girl went on, 'my father was from home and I tried to play with the children here, I tried indeed. But they were stupid, those children! The steward's brats agreed with everything I said, and the little Saxon pigs *disagreed*. It was very dull! But now you are my friends. If you mean, in truth, that you will take me with you, I should be so happy, so very happy. But how may that be done?'

Peter drew the ship from under his tunic. Matilda clapped her hands with joy. 'The little ship!' she cried. 'The little ship!' and took it upon her hand.

As she stood gazing down at the magic ship there came the sound of heavy feet ascending the steps, steel rang upon stone, and Matilda grew pale.

'It is my father,' she cried. 'Hide, oh hide!' and she pushed Sheila, who was nearest, behind the curtains that hung against the wall. The three other children dived behind, too. Matilda bent down and put the little ship upon the floor, then she shook the folds of her long gown carefully over it so that it was completely hidden. She stood still, her heart wildly beating.

The door crashed open for the second time. The fierce-eyed, eagle-nosed man stood there, scowling in the tower-room.

'There are enemies about,' he cried in a harsh grating voice. 'Robert has told me! A strange lad who speaks both the Saxon and Norman tongues. Have you seen such a lad, my child?'

Matilda stared at him with troubled eyes.

'Speak!' he commanded. 'Are you bewitched all of a sudden?'

Matilda's eyes slid here and there about the room. The angry eyes followed. With one stride the man was at the heavy curtains, plucking them apart.

The four children stood trembling beneath his fierce gaze.

'So there are four of you!' he said quite softly. 'First you shall tell me why you are here, and then I will fling you into my deepest dungeon.'

Peter said, 'Indeed, Sir—'

'Mend your manners, Saxon pig! Down on your knees!'

Peter stood upright. 'I kneel to no man,' he said proudly, 'save to my rightful king!'

The man laughed, but it was not a pleasant laugh. 'What king have you, Saxon swine? There is but one king, and for him I hold this castle!' And with a blow he sent Peter sprawling to the ground. 'You will sing much softer when I have leisure to deal with you.' He lifted a whistle that hung upon a cord at his breast, and blew a shrill blast. Instantly, it seemed, four men-at-arms stepped into the room. Heavy hands fell upon the shrinking shoulders of the children.

Down the dark stone staircase, down, down, down. It seemed to the frightened children that the journey would never come to an end. Nor did they wish it to come to an end.

At last they stood again in the court-yard. The dark sky lit by quiet stars stretched above them. The light wind stirred their hair, but neither wind nor stars could comfort their sore hearts.

'Don't stand there dreaming,' shouted one of the men, and pushed Sandy roughly. Sheila saw Peter's fists go up. 'Steady,' she whispered under her breath. He understood that he must not anger his captors further, and his hands dropped open to his side.

Across the uneven court-yard they were marched until the great wall of the castle loomed before them. A high tower went up beside the gateway, so high that, to the children, it seemed to touch the stars.

'Ay, 'tis high enough,' chuckled one of the men, 'and it is not yet finished. You may have a good look at the stars; and since it may well be your last, I advise you to look well and long!'

Two of the men herded the silent children together, while two bent and strained at a great iron ring in the ground. With much puffing and grunting they managed to lift the huge flagstone. Rough steps went down into the darkness.

'Down!' cried one of the men, and pushed the children towards the opening. There were but a few steps, and the children, standing below in the pitchy darkness, heard the sound of the flagstone dropping into place, and the heavy bolts drawn across it.

They stared into the darkness with dismay, trying in vain to catch a glimpse of each others' faces. Sandy's lip began to tremble, but the feel of Sheila's arm about her was comforting, and she decided it was too early yet to start crying.

A dark and narrow passage opened out before them and they felt their way along it. They came presently into a small square chamber with high smooth walls. The walls were so high that they could not see to the top. By stretching their heads backwards, they could see a few faint stars.

'There's no roof to this place,' Peter said hopefully.

'That doesn't help us. Nobody could possibly get out of this!' said Humphrey gloomily.

'Except birds,' added Sandy, 'I should think it reaches right up to the sky!'

'If *only* we had the ship!'

'We must never never let it out of our own hands for a single second in future,' said Peter.

'If there *is* a future!' Sheila reminded him.

'Do you think Matilda would help us?' asked Sandy anxiously.

'She would if she could. But I don't think she could do much!' said Humphrey thoughtfully.

'The brute!' said Peter rubbing his bruised shoulder.

'*Don't* let's think of him!' cried Sheila.

109

There was silence in the dark tower. Each child was thinking how different their plight would be if they held the ship safe in their hands.

Humphrey couldn't bear the dark silence any more. 'It feels as if it's going to rain,' he said, trying to make ordinary conversation.

'Oh, I don't think so,' answered Sheila in the same tone.

But even that didn't help to make the horrible black tower-prison less frightening.

There was silence again. Each child was thinking of the ugly look on the governor's face. Each was wondering what their mother and father would do when they understood at last that the children would never come home again.

It was very cold down in the black well of the tower. The children took it in turn to pace two or three steps in each direction to keep themselves from freezing.

The stars grew paler and disappeared. Staring upwards they saw the sky faintly red above the top of the tower, but in the depths where they shivered with cold it was still night.

Peter thought of the coming day. He wondered whether they would ever see another night. He wondered whether the others knew what might be in store for them. Sheila and Sandy slept huddled together for warmth on the damp ground. He was glad that they were able to sleep. Humphrey stood against the wall, his face hidden in his arm.

It grew a little lighter. A faint shaft of grey light filtered through into the tower. Just above Humphrey's head a narrow slit, a few inches wide, cut deeply into the thick stone. He stood on tip-toe to catch what he could of the fresh morning air. He kept saying to himself, 'It may be for the last time!'

Suddenly, a faint whistle sounded on the air, so faint that he could hardly believe he had really heard it. His heart was beating fit to choke him as he strained his ears to catch it again.

There was no mistake. There it was, faint and sure, like a bird's cry. And yet it was like the sound of no bird he had ever heard. He put his mouth to the slit.

'Yes?' he whispered.

'*Sh*—!' came a voice in warning.

Peter sprang towards the slit. Sheila came awake with a start, her pale face turned towards the light that filtered through the window-slit. Sandy stirred and rolled over drowsily on the hard ground.

Two dark eyes peered in through the slit. It was Matilda. She was breathless with haste and fear.

'I could not come before,' she whispered urgently. 'My father locked me in. He sent my nurse to guard me. He hung the key at her girdle. I had to wait till she was asleep. Then I stole the key. Heaven be praised, she sleeps sound! Here!'

Their hearts almost burst with joy, for in her hands she held their own magic ship.

Standing upon tip-toe she tried to push it through the narrow slit.

Their hearts sank dismally. They were sick with disappointment. The slit was too small. The ship would not pass through.

Matilda stood there, straining on tip-toe, pushing and

pushing without success. The light spread in the summer sky. The children looked about them in despair. All round them day was stirring. Birds were twittering. A cock crowed lustily. A maid was walking, rubbing her eyes, towards the well. At any moment the guard might come to the prison door.

Then Humphrey had an idea.

He reached up so that he could just touch with the tip of his finger the head of the golden boar. 'Make yourself small,' he implored, 'small enough to get through!'

'Look!' cried Matilda in astonishment.

The tiny boat was shrinking in her hand. In a moment it had slipped through the narrow slit as easily as a hot knife through butter.

Peter held it in the hollow of his hand, looking down at it in grateful wonder. Then he put it on the ground.

'Home!' he cried, his voice shaken with happiness.

The ship began to grow. As soon as they could the children stepped inside. There was just room for them to crouch huddled together. But it was enough.

'Good-bye, Matilda,' cried Peter, 'we shall never forget you!'

'We'll come back again!' cried Sheila.

Humphrey bent over as the ship began to rise. 'Will *he* punish you?' he asked.

Matilda shrugged her thin shoulders. 'Why should he punish me? I go back to lock my chamber door. He will find all as he left it. Besides—' she tried to smile a little, 'he is not always stern, but there has been much trouble lately, and it is his duty to hold the castle for our lord, King William.'

The dark cold walls of the tower sped backwards. The ship hovered over it in the early morning sunshine.

'Good-bye, good-bye, good-bye!' called the children.

'Come back, oh, do come back!' cried Matilda, brushing her hand across her eyes.

They saw her crouch against the tower wall, while the maidservant clattered across the courtyard with her wooden bucket; then, her back being turned, they saw Matilda dart swiftly across to the small door of her own tower and vanish.

And they saw something else, too, something that made them shiver in spite of the summer sunshine. Half a dozen men-at-arms marched across to the prison tower.

Then the dark cloud came down upon them, bringing them safely home once more.

CHAPTER 9

The Valley of the Kings

It was the afternoon before Christmas. The children were sitting in front of a roaring fire toasting chestnuts—and their toes. Now and again Gertrude came in with her arms full of odd-shaped parcels; she took them straight over to the cupboard which had been emptied to receive them.

'Let's have a look, do, Gertrude, be a sport!' urged Peter, but Gertrude laughingly shook her head. 'They've got to go right away till to-morrow,' she said firmly. 'That's your mother's orders!'

'She meant we weren't to look inside,' remarked Sheila, 'but that doesn't mean we can't have a peep at the labels.'

'Oh, yes it does, Miss Sheila,' said Gertrude, putting the key of the cupboard in her pocket. 'There's a lot you can tell from a label, and your mother doesn't want you to start guessing anything. Spoil everything, that would!'

'I think you're downright mean!' grumbled Humphrey.

'Very well then,' Gertrude answered, 'if that's what you think, there's a certain little parcel for a certain young gentleman, won't go in at all!'

And, as she went out at the door, she winked at Sheila to show she didn't really mean it.

'Christmas is awfully exciting!' said Humphrey.

'Yes, when it comes. But it's an awful long time coming!' added Sandy.

'We've done the paper-chains and put up the holly and packed the parcels,' Peter remarked.

'The trouble with us,' said Sheila in her most grown-up voice, 'is that we haven't enough to do!'

'All right, let's do something then,' remarked Sandy, rescuing another chestnut.

'What about another adventure?' asked Humphrey, and then added quickly, 'My turn to choose.'

'Well, choose somewhere warm!' advised Sandy, popping another chestnut into her mouth.

'I choose Egypt!' said Humphrey.

'And bang right into old Ferouz!' cried Peter. 'Not likely!'

'Egypt's a big place,' Humphrey reminded him, 'and I didn't see half the things I wanted to.'

'Ferouz or no Ferouz, it's Humphrey's turn,' declared Sheila.

'The Pyramids,' said Humphrey, 'and the tombs of the kings.'

'We'd better wrap up warm,' suggested Sheila, walking over to the window and looking at the drifting snow.

'It'll be hot in Egypt, won't it?' asked Sandy.

'I don't know. I don't expect it'll be hot anywhere on a day like this!' Humphrey said.

'Well, we'd better put on our coats and things and then we can take them off if we get too hot,' suggested Peter.

The four children ran away to get ready. Mother saw them trooping down the stairs in caps and mufflers and gloves.

'Heavens, children!' she laughed. 'You look as if you're off to the North Pole. Give Santa Claus my love!'

'We will—if we see him!' Sandy answered.

'I don't expect we shall, though,' said Humphrey truthfully.

It was very cold out of doors. Drifting snow melted on their noses and the children licked it off with their warm tongues. The wind seemed to cut through their thick clothes so that they had to run to keep themselves warm. As they came down to the shore the sea and the sky seemed to have no colour at all.

Peter drew the ship out of his pocket.

'Tell us exactly where you want to go,' he said.

'Pyramids!' replied Humphrey promptly. 'No, wait a minute, what about a rock tomb? Yes, I'd like a rock tomb—it's more uncommon!'

'I don't think I *like* tombs,' said Sandy, 'I mean they don't sound awfully cheerful.'

'These are,' Humphrey promised. 'They're awfully cheerful. You'll love them. All kinds of jolly pictures inside painted on the walls, and no end of things buried there, gold cups and plates and crowns and jewels—'

'That settles it!' cried Peter, stamping his cold feet. 'Come on!'

The children climbed over the side of the boat and Peter took his place at the prow. 'The Rock Tombs!' he cried.

Up rose the magic ship. The children smiled at each other in delight. Although they were now quite used to the ship, the smooth bird-like movement with which it lifted into the air was always delightful to them.

Sandy snuggled down at the bottom of the boat. She pulled her beret down over her nose and her scarf right up to meet it. There wasn't anything of her face to be seen, but she did look cosy, and soon the others had followed her example.

After a while Peter peered over the side of the ship. 'We're over Italy now,' he cried, 'I'm beginning to know what Europe looks like from the sky.'

'Greece!' cried Humphrey.

'The Nile!' called Peter. 'I wonder what happened to Ferouz's hat?'

'P'raps some water-birds borrowed it for a nest,' suggested Sandy.

'A much nicer use for it than being on Ferouz's nasty old head,' added Sheila, laughing.

'I bet he got a good cold that day!' said Humphrey.

'You mean a *bad* cold,' Sandy corrected him.

'Good or bad,' Humphrey answered, 'I hope he sneezed and sneezed and *sneezed*!'

The ship flew steadily on. Gradually the rice fields bordering the Nile were left behind. Great stony boulders began to thrust up through the sandy soil. Soon the ship was flying steadily over what appeared to be a rocky desert. After a while it began to slacken speed and drop.

'I'm almost sure I don't like rock tombs,' Sandy said firmly.

'You'll love them,' Humphrey encouraged her. 'I expect we'll find a gold crown for you.'

'I shall give it to mother!' Sandy said.

The ship came to ground. The children waited until she had settled herself, then they clambered out.

Up in the sky as blue as a blue-tub the fierce yellow sun beat down upon yellow rock. There was nothing to be seen anywhere but sky and rock all quivering in the fierce heat. Even Humphrey felt somewhat dashed though he did not intend to show it.

Just in front of them a low opening hewn out in the rock showed black in the shadow. Humphrey plucked up his courage. 'Come on!' he cried.

Peter followed him into the opening of the cave, but the two girls hung back. 'Come *on!*' called Peter from the shadow of the rock. 'If you hate it very much, we can always go back! I suppose,' he turned to his brother, 'you haven't got such a thing as a torch on you!'

'Yes I have,' answered Humphrey very pleased with himself. 'I thought it might be useful.'

The two boys plunged into the darkness.

'We'd better follow them,' said Sheila, 'after all, they've got the ship.' And she took Sandy by the hand.

A faint line of light fell from the torch upon the inside of the cave. 'Careful!' warned Sheila, 'there are heaps of stone and rubbish about.'

The two boys waited for them and the four children went on together.

The narrow black passage twisted and turned, but they went on steadily picking their way carefully over the rough floor of the cave. Now and again Humphrey flashed his torch upon the wall. Bright painted figures sprang into the light and the children stopped from time to time to admire them.

After a while Sheila whispered, 'Isn't the torch running out?'

Humphrey did not answer. It was not necessary, for the thread of light was growing weaker and weaker. Suddenly it went out altogether and the four children stood stock-still in the thick darkness.

Peter began to feel about him for the wall of the cave. His groping fingers brushed Sandy's shoulder and she gave a little shriek.

'It's all *right!*' exclaimed Peter a little fiercely because he couldn't help remembering, as he always did when they had got themselves into trouble, that he was the eldest. 'I'll just go on a bit and see if I can feel the way.'

'You *mustn't* go! Please!' begged Sheila. 'We simply mustn't get separated. You might get lost!'

Sandy began to cry.

'Oh, shut up!' said Peter still fiercely. And then he added more kindly, 'There's nothing to cry about.'

'Oh, isn't there?' sobbed Sandy. 'We shall never never find our way out of this horrible place, *never*, I know it! We'll go walking about in the dark, and losing our way and getting hungrier and hungrier—'

Sheila shivered in spite of herself. Her hand went out into the darkness and found Sandy's. 'No we shan't,' she said cheerfully, 'after all we've got the ship!'

'That won't help us,' sobbed Sandy, 'and you *know* it won't! It can't fly through rock, can it?'

'No, it can't,' Humphrey agreed, 'but it'll be quite easy to find our way back again. We just turn round and walk straight back the way we came.'

'Of course!' said Peter.

They turned right-about and, feeling in front of them and all about with their hands, groped their way in the pitch-black darkness.

On and on they went. In the minds of all four children the feeling was growing that they ought long ago to have reached the opening of the cave.

At last Sheila said anxiously, 'I hope we're going the right way.'

'Of course we are!' exclaimed Peter, sounding much more certain than he felt. 'You know we turned right round and came straight back.'

The passage was growing lower and lower, and now it was so low that the children had to fall on their hands and knees.

They stopped dead.

'We *must* be going wrong,' said Humphrey. 'I don't remember this at all!'

They crawled on until the passage grew higher again and they stood upright, straightening their aching backs. 'It's getting wider, too!' cried Peter. 'I can't feel the wall with my hands.'

'We're all a little tired,' said Sheila as cheerfully as she could, 'let's sit down for a little while, we'll get on much more quickly when we've had a rest.'

The four children sat down on a heap of rubble.

'Dear me! What have I in my pocket?' asked Sheila, pretending to be pleasantly surprised. 'Well now, who would have thought it? Something to eat! Pop it in your mouth and then guess what it is!'

It was a handful of chestnuts that she had slipped into her

pocket before leaving the playroom. They were hard and cold and slightly burnt, but to the tired and hungry children they were delicious.

'Now that we've had some refreshment,' Sheila went on cheerfully, 'we're going to find our way out!'

They got to their feet once more. Their eyes strained into the darkness. They could see nothing in the black cave—nothing at all but pitch-black darkness, above and below and all around. For what seemed like ages, they crept along in single file, holding on to each other with one hand, and feeling their way along the rough wall.

Suddenly Humphrey gave a loud cry. 'What's that?' he shouted, his voice quivering with excitement.

Four pairs of eyes stared eagerly round into the darkness.

'It's a light!' whispered Peter.

'It can't be,' said Sheila. 'We're just imagining it. What on earth can a light be doing here?'

'Well, what are *we* doing here, if it comes to that?' asked Humphrey.

'It's a ghost or something,' said Sandy, trembling.

'Don't be so silly!' Humphrey said. 'Ghosts don't go about carrying lanterns with them. Besides, there aren't such things! I expect we're not the only people in the world that are interested in rock tombs.'

'I shouldn't be surprised if we are!' retorted Sandy.

They watched the glimmer of light a moment longer and then Peter raised his voice.

'Hull-oo-oo!'

The echo of his own voice came back weirdly in the empty cave.

'The ghost's laughing at us!' whispered Sandy, shivering.

'Don't be such a little idiot, for heaven's sake!' cried Peter. 'Don't you know an echo when you hear one? Now then let's all call out together.'

'Hull-oo-oo!'

Four voices sent the sound ringing through the empty darkness.

'Hull-oo-oo!' came back faintly, but this time it was no echo but the unmistakable sound of a man's voice.

'Sta-ay where you a-are!' called the voice. It was far distant, but the children could just make out the words. They sat down again, straining their eyes to watch the faint beam.

'The light's getting brighter!' said Humphrey after a little while.

'And wider!' added Peter.

A broad beam of light travelled through the cave. The four children sprang up joyfully and hastened towards it. Sandy fell head-first upon a comfortable stomach.

'Hold hard!' said the owner of the stomach. He shifted his lamp into the left hand and caught hold of Sandy with the right. Then he flashed his lamp upon the little group. He stood staring down at the children as if he could hardly believe his eyes.

'Good Lord!' he exclaimed at last. 'I must be dreaming!'

'No, we're quite real,' said Humphrey. 'You can pinch us if you like!'

Sandy withdrew her hand and edged away from the stranger with the lamp.

'I won't do that!' he exclaimed, laughing. It was the kind of laugh that belongs to a really nice person, and the children felt comforted.

'Well, you know,' said the man with the lamp, 'this *is* rather a surprise!'

'A very pleasant one for us!' answered Sheila with feeling.

'I dare say it is!' remarked the man with the lamp, somewhat grimly. 'Where are the rest of you?'

Peter shook his head. 'There's only us,' he said.

'Four children alone! How you got here beats me! Well, the first thing is to get out of this and then we can talk!'

The fierce light of his acetylene lamp threw their shadows dancing weirdly over the walls of the cave. But now the children were no longer frightened. Following in the footsteps of their new friend, they felt that their adventure was really beginning at last. The narrow path twisted and turned. Once again they were all forced to their hands and knees. On and on they went. Suddenly Sheila gave a glad cry and pointed to a faint grey patch in the distance.

'Yes, daylight!' said the man with the lamp. 'Nice, isn't it?'

Ten minutes steady walking brought them at last to the entrance of the cave. Once more they stood in the fresh air. The sunlight was so dazzling that they were forced to shut their eyes for a little while.

'Well!' said their new friend. 'We can't possibly talk here! You'd better come over to the tent and we'll get things straight.'

Sandy slipped her hand in his. She thought he was the nicest person she had ever met. From time to time the older children would steal a glance at their new friend. Peter thought that the thin sunburnt face with the bright blue eyes was the cleverest he had ever seen, and Humphrey was sure it was the kindest. Sheila walked along knitting her brows. What explanation were they going to give? She was worried. Their new friend had a kind face, certainly, but the chin didn't look as though it would stand any nonsense; and the blue eyes looked keen enough to see through any untruth. Besides, he wasn't the kind of person that one would want to tell untruths to! Of course, Sheila thought, one should *never* want to tell untruths—

She brushed the damp hair back from her forehead.

Under a ledge of rock, protected from the fiercest rays of the sun, stood a tent, and the new-comer led the way towards it.

It was extremely neat inside. The main piece of furniture was a deal table, very white and clean, on which stood a handsome microscope. It was stacked up with books, papers, pencils, paints and paintbrushes, compasses and other geometrical instruments, several silk dusters, and a couple of magnifying-glasses.

The stranger pushed several packing-cases forward. 'Sit down and make yourselves comfortable,' he said. 'Honestly, I can't get over this! First of all you'd better tell me something about yourselves and then we'll have something to eat!'

'Hooray!' cried Sandy. The others were far too polite to cheer, but the prospect of food was very pleasant.

'Well,' began Peter. 'Our names are Peter—that's me.

And Humphrey—that's him. And Sheila—' he nodded towards her. 'And the one hanging over your shoulder like the old man of the sea is Sandy.'

'I'm not hanging on!' cried Sandy indignantly. 'Am I?'

'Of course not!' agreed their new friend. 'Well, now I know your names! But what I really want to know is what you're doing here!'

'Well, we wanted to see a rock-tomb—' Humphrey explained, and stopped. He did not see how he could possibly explain to a reasonable grown-up about the magic ship.

'So you managed to slip away from your parents?' asked the stranger, taking it for granted that their parents must be near at hand. 'Well, how you managed to find your way here beats me. It beats me hollow! Well, you *are* here, and I'm pleased to see you, for I was getting a bit tired of my own company. I hope your parents aren't worrying too much about you, and later on you can tell me just how to return you. Now I suppose I'd better introduce myself. After all,' his eyes twinkled, 'you can't be too particular what company you keep. My name is Nickalls. John Nickalls.'

There came a little gasp from Humphrey.

'Not *the* John Nickalls,' he breathed. 'Not really!'

The stranger nodded. 'The very same! How do you know about me?'

'Oh, *sir*!' cried Humphrey. 'Everybody knows about you! I do anyway, because I mean to be an arky—arky—I can spell it, but I can't say it!'

'Archaeologist! Well, I can say it but I can't spell it,' confessed Nickalls, laughing.

Humphrey turned to the others. 'It's the one who found a new temple last year, in some pyramid or other. I can't remember the name. I read all I could about it because of being so interested, because of wanting to be an arky—well, the word you can't spell!'

John Nickalls rose from his packing-case and bowed gravely.

'Now you know I'm respectable,' he said, 'what about something to eat?'

'Hooray!' cried all the children together, feeling that by now their new friend had become a very old one.

Soon every one was very busy. Peter and Humphrey were dragging several packing-cases together to serve as a table since John Nickalls didn't want his papers moved. Sheila was busy hacking slices off a loaf, John Nickalls was opening tins of tongue and sardines and pineapple, while Sandy arranged them artistically on the 'table'.

When everything was ready they each sat down on a packing-case. Every one was hungry, and never had pineapple and sardines and tongue tasted so good. When at last they had finished, Peter stood up and made a little speech. 'Mr. Nickalls, ladies and gentlemen,' he said, 'we've all had a lovely meal and we want to thank Mr. Nickalls for saving our lives, because I don't think we should ever have found our way out of that awful cave. So now we will all sing *For He's a Jolly Good Fellow*.'

They sang with such heartiness that the walls of the tent quivered. When they had finished singing, John Nickalls stood up to thank them. 'Ladies and gentlemen,' he said,

'Thank you for your beautiful speech and for your beautiful singing. I don't know which I liked best. Now what would you like to do?'

Humphrey said, 'I did terribly want to see the inside of a rock-tomb, I mean the really-truly tomb part. I wish— p'raps—I mean would it be too much to ask you to show us things?'

'Of course I will. But first let me tell you about it. When I found you, you were in the king's chamber. That's where the sarcophagus—'

'The *what*?' asked Sandy.

'That long word means the case that held the king's body. Well, that has gone along with the mummy to the museum at Cairo. It was a marvellous thing, inlaid heavily with gold. You know the mummy-case always bears the portrait of the person inside. Well, this picture of the king was as clear as if it had been painted only yesterday. And a fine looking chap he was!'

'Did you find any treasure?' asked Peter.

'The ordinary things. Cups and plates of gold, and a crown. And slipped in between the linen folds of the bandages round the body we found several jewels.'

'O-oh!' breathed Sheila and Sandy together.

'I suppose young ladies would think crowns and jewels quite the most interesting things, but they weren't, not by long chalks. There was something much more interesting, something that brings me back day after day, although the expedition is finished for this year, at any rate, and the men paid off. All the treasure has been carried away and is now

127

neatly set out in a museum, and yet—that something keeps me working in the cave itself. I can't keep away from it.'

'What is it?' asked Humphrey in a breathless sort of voice.

'You wouldn't understand,' said Nickalls slowly. 'It's all so curious that I haven't dared mention it to any one.'

Then seeing the eager faces turned towards him he said, 'Well, you see the coffin-lid has an inscription round it that I can't make out. At least, I can make out the hieroglyphics—the picture letters you know—but they don't make sense. It's so queer that I feel I *must* be mistaken, and yet I simply can't see where the mistake comes in.'

The children were listening intently and John Nickalls went on, 'The inscription keeps mentioning a ship—a flying-ship.'

He could feel the children stiffen with excitement, and he continued,

'Well, now, a flying-ship isn't so curious, in a way. The Egyptians believed in magic and they practised it, too. Wonderful things they did. You've only got to look in your Bible to find out.'

'Like Moses and Aaron before Pharaoh and the rods and serpents and things!' said Sheila.

Nickalls nodded.

'Now if the ship had been the *ordinary* pattern of an Egyptian ship, I shouldn't have thought twice about it. The ship of Osiris—that's one of their chief gods, or the Sunboat of Ra—that's another god—well, you might expect that. But it isn't. It's something quite different. It's the kind of ship you find a couple of thousand years later in a very different kind of land. A dragon-ship, complete with square sails and a gilt boar's head at the prow.'

The four children sat perfectly still, staring at Nickalls. Each wanted to speak, but no one knew what to say. It was queer sitting there in the shadowed tent, hearing about their ship, their very own ship.

'A dragon-ship of all things!' Nickalls went on. 'Why, it's as fantastic as finding a speed-boat carved by men of the Old Stone Age! It beats me!'

Peter found his voice at last, but it was rather a quavering voice. 'Are you quite, quite sure?' he asked.

'Quite!' answered Nickalls, and his voice was very definite. 'I'll show it to you presently. There's a story, too,' he added.

'Oh!' cried the four children together, and Sandy gave his arm an excited pinch.

'It sounds as if you'd like to hear it,' laughed Nickalls. 'And a queer tale it is! As I said, although the inscriptions are plain enough, they don't always make good sense. Still, if you'd like to hear it—'

'*Rather!*' cried the four children, and settled themselves comfortably to listen.

'Well, it seems that when King Usertsen was a lad, his father went off to fight. His father was Amenemhat the First, a wise man and a strong king. And he had need to be both, I can tell you, because he had enemies within and without. First of all there were the great nobles who during the reigns of the last weak kings had got used to doing exactly what they pleased. And outside his kingdom he was surrounded by enemies, Ethiopians and Libyans, who raided the country whenever they got the chance. They were troubled times for Egypt and the king had to fight for his throne, and fight hard. In fact, he was so hard pressed that he had to leave the capital, Thebes, and he moved with all his court to a tiny little place called Lisht, which wasn't so magnificent but a good deal safer.

'Now his chief enemy at the time were the Nubians—the Ethiopians as they were called. They were fierce and wild and strong. They hid among the desert rocks and attacked the caravans as they passed into Egypt. They took the gold and ivory and rare spices and murdered the Egyptians. And then they grew bolder and bolder and no one knew when the Nubians might not fall upon them, their daggers red with blood, their eyes wild with victory.

'Well, Pharaoh went off to settle the business once and for all. He took with him his generals and his picked soldiers, and his slaves and his elephants and his wild beasts—'

'And his chariots and horses,' added Sandy.

'No, not horses and chariots; there weren't any horses in Egypt until much later, and at this time they didn't fight from chariots. He left his little son Usertsen behind him to govern his people.'

'How could a little boy do that?' asked Sandy.

'Well, of course, he couldn't. The priests and ministers would do that for him. But Usertsen was there to remind the people that they had to behave in the absence of Pharaoh and that everything had to go on just as if he were there.

'And it was a good thing Usertsen *was* there, as you'll see.

'Well, every one expected the king to return in a very short time. And of course victorious. I expect the artists and stone-masons got busy the very day of his departure to get the story of the latest victory carved on the temple walls so that Amenemhat should be able to read about it as soon as he returned. You see, the carvings on the temples were a sort of history-book and newspaper in one.

'Prince Usertsen was just as certain as every one else, because his father was a famous fighter, and as brave as one of his own fighting lions, and he had taken the pick of the armed forces with him. Besides—it was a surprise raid, and that would make it all the more certain.

'And then something happened that made him not so certain.'

John Nickalls stopped to take breath. The four children sat there utterly still, without moving a muscle, while he went on with his tale.

'It seems that he overheard a conversation between the High Priest and the Chief Minister which showed him without any doubt that they had betrayed the king and sold him into the hands of his enemy.

'You can imagine how he felt. There was his father marching straight into the trap and there was nothing any one could do about it. And he must have known, if he'd stopped to think about it, that it would be the end of things for himself, too!

'All that part, about the fight with the Nubians and the betrayal and so on, is quite straightforward. It falls into its proper place in the history of Ancient Egypt. You can read about it on the monuments and temples that Amenemhat left behind. But this is where the mystery begins, this is where I can't really believe that the inscriptions mean what they appear to.

'The flying-ship comes into the story.

'The inscription tells us that a flying-ship appeared to Usertsen with four gods inside and that these gods delivered the king from the hand of his enemy. How, when, and where, it doesn't say. Just that. No more!

'Usertsen ordered an inscription to be made testifying to the truth of the story, and placed upon his coffin. He also ordered that it should be carved into the rock so that it would endure for all time. Odd, isn't it?'

The four children stared at each other. Words failed them. There was simply nothing they could say.

'Awfully queer!' breathed Peter at last.

'And now I've told you so much,' said John Nickalls, smiling, 'I'll tell you one thing more. When I found you in the cave, a queer thing happened. There were four of you—and it gave me a sort of shock. Almost as if I'd, well, as if I'd stumbled right into the middle of the story, and as if the flying-ship was somewhere near. That comes of working too hard, I suppose! Let me warn you,' and here he twinkled, 'against working too hard! And now—' he looked at his watch, 'it's time I was getting back. There's just time to see the picture in the cave if you want to!'

'Rather!' cried three voices together. Sandy looked a little doubtful. 'If you'll hold my hand all the time!' she said at last.

He held out his hand with a smile. 'Promise!' he said.

132

They set off briskly and soon they had passed into the black mouth of the cave. John Nickalls flashed his bright lamp ahead and the children recognized the pictured walls they had seen before. After a little while the path branched to left and right, and they followed a wide, smooth path hewn out of the living rock.

'You took the path to the left,' Nickalls said. 'They both lead to the King's Chamber, but no one could possibly have carried a sarcophagus that way. You had to get down on your hands and knees, remember?'

They remembered only too well.

A few minutes quick walking brought them to the great cave where John Nickalls had found them. Now he led them up to a wall which had been chiselled smooth. He held up his lamp so that the wall was flooded with light. 'There!' he cried. 'What do you think of that?'

The children stood speechless, staring at the picture of their own ship. It was a faithful picture, the colours bright and the shape true. Staring at it, the children had an uneasy feeling, almost as if they expected, at any moment, a hand to drop upon their shoulder. Peter's hand went to his pocket to feel if his ship was indeed there. It was. Thankfully his fingers closed on it.

'Well now,' said Nickalls, 'you've seen it! And what's more, you've seen what nobody else has, except myself, so you must promise to say nothing about it for at least six months. My book will be out then and I shan't mind.'

To his surprise the four children crossed their fingers, and lightly touching hands chanted the following verse,

133

Earth and water and fire and air,
We solemnly promise, we solemnly swear,
Not a word nor a look nor a sound to declare,
Earth and water and fire and air!

'Now I *do* feel safe!' declared Nickalls, smiling. 'Well, we really must be going. I've enjoyed myself so much that I've made myself frightfully late!'

Ten minutes later they stood at the entrance of the cave, and once again they were forced to shut their eyes in the strong sunlight. At last, when they could see again quite plainly, the children held out their hands in farewell.

'Good-bye, and thank you, thank you, *thank* you!' they cried together.

'Not so fast!' exclaimed John Nickalls. 'You don't suppose I'm going to leave you children alone all among the rock-tombs. Why, you might break your ankles or necks or anything!'

'But we have to go home!' explained Peter.

'Exactly. And I'm going to see you get there! I shouldn't get a wink of sleep in a month of Sundays unless I handed you over myself to your parents. What's the name of your hotel?'

The children looked at each other blankly.

'Well, never mind,' said Nickalls cheerfully 'we'll find it when we get there. Now look here, don't make any more fuss. Here's my Rolls-Royce,' and he pointed to a battered Ford that stood blistering in the fierce sunshine. 'Hop inside. I'm staying in Thebes—and of course you must be, too. When we get there you can tell me which way to go.'

Rather unhappily the children climbed into the car. Nickalls followed them. He sat there with one hand on the steering-wheel and the other fumbling in the pocket of his white suit.

'Bother!' he said. 'I've left my pipe somewhere. I remember lighting it when we were looking at the ship in the cave! Sorry, but you'll have to wait while I get it. It's a favourite you see, and I couldn't enjoy my evening without it.' And he got out again.

As soon as he had disappeared into the mouth of the cave Peter said quickly, 'Now!' They scrambled out of the car and Peter put his boat on the ground.

'Home!' he cried.

The children stood sadly, waiting for the ship to grow.

'It *is* a rotten way to behave!' said Sheila, sighing.

'I know!' Peter agreed, 'but what can we *do*?'

'He's *sweet*!' said Sandy.

Humphrey said nothing. He was thinking that John Nickalls must be quite the finest person in the world, and it was dreadful running away from him the minute his back was turned.

Still there was nothing else to be done! Now the ship was large enough to hold them, and they stepped inside.

John Nickalls, emerging, pipe in hand, from the cave, cast a quick look at his car. It was empty. 'Stop fooling!' he cried aloud, but only his own echo came back from the empty air. He looked about him with puzzled eyes, and then, then he saw something that made those eyes almost start from his head.

The ship. The flying-ship of the inscription, complete with glowing boar's head, rose slowly into the air with the four children inside.

'I'm not seeing it! I can't be!' he told himself as he walked slowly towards the car. 'I've got that confounded ship on the brain. And the children, too! I must have imagined them. Finding them like that in the cave—four of them, exactly as in the story. It's utterly fantastic. That's what it is, fantastic! I need a holiday, and, by Jove, I mean to take one!'

He stared once more up at the hard blue sky. Four white handkerchiefs waved as the ship rose.

'It can't be! It *can't* be!' he murmured, feeling in his pocket, and, as his own handkerchief waved in response, he asked himself, 'And yet, can't it? *Can't* it?'

CHAPTER 10

To the Time of Usertsen

Christmas was over and the children's presents were no longer new. Boxing Day, too, had come and gone with its excitement of party clothes and a visit to the pantomime. No wonder that the days following Christmas Day and Boxing Day were rather dull!

The children were in the playroom as usual. Sandy was making coconut ice for all of them in a little saucepan over the fire. But as she kept tasting it every minute or so, Humphrey asked a little anxiously whether she were having her share now.

Humphrey and Peter were poring over their stamp albums. Peter had started his last year, and Humphrey had only started his these holidays; in fact his handsome green and gold album had been Gertrude's Christmas present. Peter had a great deal of information to pass on to Humphrey, and Humphrey was glad to listen. Every now and then Peter would give Humphrey a stamp to stick in the new green and gold album, and then Humphrey was gladder than ever.

Sheila was knitting away for dear life. She was making an oven-cloth because cook had run out of them and cook had promised her a chocolate cake for tea if she hurried up with it. Cook always said you couldn't beat Miss Sheila's knitting.

There was silence in the room, broken by the sudden sound of argument.

'Look out!' cried Peter. 'You're putting that stamp in the wrong place!'

'I'm not!' declared Humphrey in his worst arguing voice. 'I think it looks pretty where it is!'

'You don't have to make it look *pretty*!' answered Peter scornfully. 'You've got to stick it in the right place, fathead!'

'I'll put them where I jolly well like!' said Humphrey obstinately. 'It's *my* album!'

'Is the coconut ice ready?' interrupted Sheila, changing the conversation.

'I don't know!' Sandy was doubtful.

Sheila put down her knitting and came over to the fire. The mixture in the saucepan didn't look very attractive. It didn't even look very much like coconut ice. Smuts from the fire had fallen into it, and the grey-looking mess had been prodded into bumps and hollows by Sandy's inquiring finger.

'It hasn't set yet,' Sheila remarked, not wishing to hurt Sandy's feelings.

'That doesn't matter, it tastes jolly good,' said Sandy eagerly. 'Don't let's wait any longer. I love it hot! Look after it for me while I go for some spoons. Don't let those boys touch it while I'm gone or there won't be a spot left.'

In a moment she was back again with four plates and four spoons. She proceeded to divide it as fairly as she could. 'Only bags I the scrapings because I made it!' she said.

Sandy was right. In spite of its appearance it certainly did taste good!

'What are we going to do now?' she asked, scraping the saucepan and licking the last crumb from the spoon.

'What about another adventure?' asked Peter.

'Good!' cried Humphrey.

'Well, I'm glad we agree about something!' returned Peter.

'Where shall we go?' asked Sheila, throwing down her knitting.

'Anywhere!' cried Sandy, waving her spoon about. 'As long as we don't get lost in horrid dark caves!'

'It wasn't so bad. It was rather fun, really!' said Humphrey.

'Well, I don't like that kind of fun!' declared Sandy firmly.

There was silence while the children sat thinking where they would like to go. Suddenly Humphrey cried, 'I've got it!' The three others looked up inquiringly, and he went on eagerly, 'You remember Nickalls telling us about the flying-ship—you know, the one in the picture-writing?'

'I should jolly well think I do! I can't get it out of my head!' declared Peter. He took his ship out of his pocket and stroked it lovingly.

'Well it *is* rum, as Nickalls said. Let's go back and find out exactly what *did* happen!'

'Rather!' cried Peter. 'Chariots and soldiers and battles! Top-hole!'

'Not chariots,' Sheila reminded him. 'The Egyptians hadn't thought of them, John Nickalls said so!'

'It's my turn to choose again,' cried Sandy, 'and I don't like fighting and battles and things.'

'There'll be lots of other things to see,' Peter assured her. 'You needn't go near a battle if you don't want to!'

'You'll be able to go inside a real palace,' Sheila pointed out, 'and you can play with the princesses while we go and have a look at the battle. There's sure to be lots of princesses about because I believe the Egyptians had harems. And there'll be lots of lovely things to eat.'

'Do you think so?' asked Sandy, brightening up.

'Sure to be!' said Humphrey quickly.

'All right!' Sandy said at last. 'I don't suppose the battles will be so bad! I'm not going to be left behind in a stuffy old palace while the rest of you go flying off in the ship!'

'I don't think we ought to separate,' Peter agreed. 'Come on! Let's hurry up!'

Wrapped up warmly in their winter things the children trooped downstairs. The beach was quite empty when they arrived, and they did not wait to reach their cove before Peter drew out the magic ship.

'Egypt!' he cried. 'To the time of Amenemhat the First!'

Up went the ship straight as an arrow. Then on the clear sky, like a smudge from a giant's finger, appeared the familiar black cloud.

'I'm always thrilled when I see that cloud,' remarked Sheila. 'It's marvellous to know that you're going to come down on the other side of history.'

'I don't like it at all!' declared Sandy, shivering a little as it raced towards them. 'It's black and it's cold and I can't help wondering whether we shall ever get through it!'

'Don't be so silly,' Peter assured her. 'As long as we've got the magic boat we're all right.'

By this time the cloud was upon them. They had not remembered it was so thick and dark, and even Sheila shivered a little in spite of her brave words.

High up in the sky the magic ship hung motionless, wrapped about in the thick cloud. Time seemed endless to the children as they crouched in the darkness. Humphrey flashed his torch and they looked into one another's pale faces.

'It isn't going to clear!' said Peter at last. 'The magic's running out.' He glanced about him. 'Like the battery of Humphrey's torch!'

'O-o-oh!' wailed Sandy, and hid her head in Sheila's lap.

Humphrey said quickly, 'It's all right, really it is! I've been working it out. The farther you go back, the longer the cloud lasts and the thicker it is. That's only sense!'

'Do you *really* think so? True honour?' asked Sandy's muffled voice.

'True honour!' Humphrey assured her. 'You can work it out for yourself. When we went to see Matilda we went back only about eight hundred years. And when we went to Asgard, that was farther back in time and the cloud lasted longer. Don't you remember how bothered we were?'

Sheila and Peter nodded.

'Well, this is the farthest we've ever gone!' exclaimed Humphrey, 'and that's why the cloud is lasting all this time!'

'Look!' cried Peter in excitement. 'It's thinning ! You *were* right, Huff!'

The children laughed in sheer relief; even Humphrey was relieved, for he had been by no means certain that he was right. It was just possible that the magic *had* run out, as Peter said. After all, you knew a lot less about magic than you did about an electric torch.

Soon the ship was winging its proud way through the clear, bright sky. The pale winter sun shone on the gleaming head of the golden boar. It was exciting, peering down over the side of the ship on to the country outspread below.

It was England and yet not England. The same. Yet different.

'The Thames!' cried Humphrey as they flew over a winding ribbon of water.

'Can't be!' argued Peter. 'Look at all those marshes and thick forests. Heaven knows where we are, but we're nowhere near the Thames.'

'Oh yes we are!' Humphrey told him. 'See that bunch of huts built on a sort of pier over the water, well that's London. The very first London there ever was, just as it tells you in history books.'

On went the ship.

It was France and yet not France. Italy and yet not Italy. There were neither towns nor villages, only marshes and dense forests and wild beasts.

Over Italy and Greece—though everything was so different that the children were no longer sure of anything.

'Look!' cried Sheila, pointing at what appeared in the distance to be a city. 'First marshes and wild beasts, and now a city with temples and palaces. It seems as if we're dodging about in time.'

Peter followed her pointing finger. 'It certainly *is* a city,' he admitted, 'and I don't understand it either. We've never dodged about like this before, we've always gone back to one certain time and stayed there.'

Humphrey said slowly, 'I remember reading that the Egyptians knew all sorts of things, you know, about building and writing, and making drains even, when the Britons roamed like savages over the marshes of Britain. Funny isn't it, to see History come alive under your eyes?'

Sheila nodded, her eyes on the white city that was gradually drawing nearer.

'Look!' cried Humphrey. 'The pyramids!'

'Gracious!' exclaimed Peter. 'They look as red and as new as if they've only just been finished.'

'Perhaps they have!' said Sandy.

The green water of the Nile welcomed them back with the face of a familiar friend. Now the ship began to fly low. Very slowly it dropped to earth, and each child in climbing out passed a hand over the head of the golden boar.

Then they stood quite still, staring at each other.

'You *do* look funny!' giggled Sandy.

'You ought to see yourself!' retorted Sheila.

'I expect it's the pot calling the kettle black,' said Peter. He began to laugh. 'And how black!'

Humphrey's voice came out, high with surprise. 'We're different. Quite different!'

And indeed it was true.

All four were dressed alike—or at least undressed alike, since they wore a very short pleated kilt of fine linen and nothing else upon their bare brown bodies. Their black shining hair was cut across their forehead in a square fringe, under which their dark eyes stared at each other in amazement.

'I'm not even sure which is which,' said Peter. 'Let me see! I'm me, of course, and that's Sandy because she's the fattest. And that's Sheila because she's the biggest. So I suppose the creature in the middle must be Humphrey.'

'Creature yourself!' cried Humphrey indignantly. 'Look here, do you want a black eye?'

Peter began to laugh. He was laughing so much that he could not stop himself. '*You* don't want a black eye!' he said when he could speak at last. 'You've got two beauties already.'

'What on earth do you mean?' asked Humphrey.

'Look at the others and you'll see!' chuckled Peter.

'You don't mean to say I look like those two!' cried Humphrey.

'Heavens!' exclaimed Sheila. 'Do I look like him?'

'Exactly!' Peter nodded, still grinning. 'We all do!'

'I like the look of me if I look like him!' cried Sandy, and began to dance on bare brown feet.

They marched sturdily along. It was very hot indeed, but the thick black hair hanging to their shoulders protected the back of their necks from the sun, and their bare bodies gave them a delightful sense of freedom.

'Lovely, lovely adventure!' cried Sandy, dancing up and down.

'You didn't want to come,' Peter reminded her.

'I do now!' cried Sandy, still dancing up and down.

The four children swung along the hot and dusty road. Once they passed an old man driving his goats, and once a young boy met them full in the middle of the road driving a flock of geese. The creatures stretched out their long necks and hissed wildly so that Sandy hid hastily behind Peter, while the boy, scratching his sunburnt neck, cackled louder than any goose.

At last they came to the gates of the city. The inward-sloping walls of sunbaked brick stood before them. They had not noticed the walls before because they were drab and low.

'The white city we passed was much grander than this,' said Sheila. 'It had palaces and temples on each side of the river. I should have thought the king would live there!'

'Well, he doesn't!' said Peter.

The four children walked boldly through and no one questioned them as they wandered about the dusty streets. It was a dull-looking town, for the streets, also of sunbaked brick, ran straight as though they had been ruled. Of houses and gardens there was not a sign; the drab walls went up, wall upon wall.

It was very quiet in the streets. Men, women, and children went by; some wore wide straw hats, others gaily striped head-cloths, but those who seemed of higher rank wore wigs of thick, stiffly greased curls to protect them from the sun.

At last they came into the market-place. Here, too, it was quieter than any market-place had a right to be. There were plenty of women and old men gossiping about the booths, and children playing, but of young and active men they saw few.

145

'It's like an old lady's town,' said Peter. 'It doesn't seem natural!'

'I expect that's because of the fighting,' said Humphrey. 'Nickalls told us about it, remember.'

They wandered on, feeling slightly depressed because their great adventure seemed to be falling flat. Where were the soldiers, and the banners, and the coloured tents? Their feet trailed a little in the red dust, and they came to a standstill before a great wall of granite. Two marble sphinxes guarded the immense pylons; between them a massive doorway of decorated copper stood open. Peeping inside they caught a glimpse of an enormous pillared courtyard.

'I suppose that's the palace,' said Sandy. 'It's the grandest building we've seen so far!'

'I expect it is,' Peter agreed.

'Let's ask,' suggested Sheila.

'I don't like asking,' replied Humphrey. 'It *shows* we're strangers, and the country's at war.'

But he was too late. Sandy had darted away and was already inquiring.

The woman stared at them with wide-open eyes.

'Hey?' she cried in so loud and shrill a voice that from nowhere a crowd had collected and gathered about them. 'Are you heathen or crazy folk that you do not know a temple when you see one? Or,' with a quick suspicious look, 'maybe you are foreigners.'

'Foreigners! Foreigners!' came in angry voices from the ever-thickening crowd.

And now an uglier word was being shouted into the air.

'Spies! Spies!' A man put his fingers in his mouth and blew a shrill whistle. He looked odd standing there, his fingers stretching his mouth wide, but none of the children felt inclined to laugh.

'Here be foreigners and spies!' cried the woman Sandy had questioned as two watchmen came running. She was big with her own importance. 'They creep into our city to steal our plans and betray us to our death!'

'Cast them into prison!'

'To the crocodiles!'

'To the torture!'

'Flay them! Burn them!'

The ugly cries came thick and fast. The children stood quiet and frightened and bewildered. The guards dropped rough hands upon their shoulders. Peter tried to wrench himself free from those strong hands. 'We haven't done anything wrong,' he cried, hoping that his voice did not betray his fear. 'We haven't done anything wrong, so you can't do anything to us!'

'Oh, can't we?' grinned one of the men, and he tightened his grip on Peter's shoulder so that the boy winced with pain.

'No, you can't!' cried Peter as loudly as he could. 'Take us before your king and let him judge!'

'Our king is many a day's journey hence, as you would know if you were not foreign spies.'

'Then take us before whoever is governing in his place!' Peter demanded.

The two men stood looking at each other as if wondering what to do.

'If any man demand audience of Pharaoh, it must be granted,' said the first guard at last.

'Nay!' screeched the woman who had caused all the trouble. 'Pharaoh is not within the city. Lock them fast in prison so that we may be safe, we and our children, while our husbands are away!'

'The prince sits in Pharaoh's place,' said the second guard slowly. 'They must go before him. It is the law of the land and we dare not disobey!'

The four children were hustled roughly through the streets, followed by the jeering, angry crowd. At last they came to the palace gates.

'Your business?' demanded the soldier on guard, pointing his spear.

'These seek audience of Pharaoh!' cried the guard, grinning and jerking his great thumb in contempt.

'Indeed! And does Pharaoh seek audience with these dogs?' cried the soldier, grinning in his turn, but he let them through.

They were pushed before the guards into a great court-yard. It was full of bustle and gay with colour. Slaves were coming and going with water-jars balanced upon their heads, or carrying great baskets of fruit or trays of meat. A boy went by with a leopard on a strong chain, the beast snarling and showing his teeth. Dragged along roughly, they passed through an inner court supported by stone pillars that cast a pleasant shade. Brilliant flowers in wooden tubs gave richness and warmth to the cool stone. The children would have been glad to stop for a minute to take breath; besides, they were desperately anxious to discuss what they should tell the prince. What on earth could they say to make him believe in their innocence? But the guards pulled them angrily along.

'Pharaoh you asked for and Pharaoh you shall have!' said one.

'And lucky you will be if the Lion of Justice does not tear you to rags before you can open your mouths!' said the other, grinning widely.

The children did not understand and they walked on quietly between their captors. At last they came to an inner door. This, too, was guarded by men-at-arms, but at the sight of the guards they lowered their spears and the children passed through.

CHAPTER 11

The Lion of Justice

They found themselves in an enormous hall with high pillars supporting the roof. The floor was paved with mosaics of coloured stone, and at one end stood a throne of gold. On the throne sat a boy with a great yellow dog at his side. The boy wore a circlet of gold from which a golden cobra reared itself, showing its fangs. He wore a kilt like that of the children, and a broad collar of precious stones upon his bare chest. One brown hand lay lightly upon the head of the great yellow dog, the other held in his lap a lash with a handle of gold. He held it as a king holds a sceptre, which indeed it was.

The boy appeared sunk in thought, and judging by the droop of his shoulders his thoughts were not pleasant.

The four children stopped dead in their tracks and the boy looked upon them coldly.

'I will see no more to-day!' he said in a weary voice. 'All this day I have listened to the petitions of my people, and now the audience is at an end!'

The two guards fell flat upon their faces.

'Pharaoh has spoken!' they said together.

'Yet, traitors and spies though they be,' said the first, 'they yet have right to Pharaoh's judgement. If Pharaoh will judge no more to-day, I will hold them safe till Pharaoh again hold audience.'

Peter jerked his shoulder free and took a step forward. The boy on the throne sat very upright. The two boys looked each other steadily between the eyes. At last, with a gesture the young prince commanded the watch to be gone and they hurried away as fast as their trembling legs would carry them—for they had no mind to remain for what was to come.

Very deliberately, his eyes still on Peter, the boy loosed his hold of the dog's collar. The great creature lifted his head, and behold, it was no dog, but a lion with a collar of bright metal about its neck.

Peter, returning the steady gaze of the prince, noticed nothing, but the three other children stood stiff with horror. The great lion threw back its head, stared out of his amber eyes and then dropped his head again into the prince's hand.

A faint smile passed over the prince's face. 'The Lion of Justice has spoken,' he said, 'and you are free!' He struck upon a silver gong and a slave stood bowed before him.

'Bid the Keeper of the Lions take charge of Buru,' he commanded, and beckoned the children nearer. The great lion crouched, his head upon his paws, still as a lion in stone.

'He would not touch a hair of your heads now he has accepted you,' said the boy, 'Now we speak freely as friend to friend. Tell me whence you come.'

'We come from very far away,' said Peter. 'Our home is across the sea.'

He stopped. The prince looked steadily at him, desiring to hear more, so Peter continued.

151

'Our land is not like your land,' he said, and stopped. Then, seeing that the prince was waiting, he went on slowly. 'Our skies are not so blue—nor the sun so bright. And the wind is often rough and cold, and the sea is wild and fierce. But—' his head went up, 'it is a fine land, and it is called England.'

'England!' repeated the prince, musing. 'It is a name I never heard. Have you great cities?'

'Not as big as yours,' said Sandy thinking of Radcliff village.

The prince smiled sadly. 'Ah, you should see my Thebes, Thebes of the Hundred Gates, with the temples and palaces lying white on either side the green river. But we had to leave Thebes because of the enemy that attacked us from all sides. But one day we shall go back. My father shall sit upon the high throne at Thebes and I with him.'

Suddenly his face clouded.

'My father will never sit upon the throne at Thebes,' he said, 'never again!' And he turned away his head.

'Why do you say that?' asked Sheila. 'The fighting isn't over yet, is it?'

'The fighting is not yet begun,' answered the boy.

'Your father is brave, isn't he?' asked Humphrey.

'The bravest in the world,' replied the boy proudly. 'But no man may stand against treachery!'

He stopped and would say no more, for the Keeper of the Lions had stepped into the hall, and the prince waited, until, holding fast to Buru, the man had bowed himself away.

'You must know,' he said, 'that my father is in the

Ethiopian desert, and all the army with him, for the Ethiopians do great wrong to our land; they plunder our caravans and slaughter our people. The Libyans, too, are our enemy, and my father thought to teach them all a lesson. So he collected great tribute and gathered together his generals and his captains and his soldiers and his slaves, and the wild beasts, too, that work great havoc. On this fight he stakes all. If he should fail—'

The boy opened his hands and let them fall.

'If he fails?' asked Peter.

'Then they will swarm into our land and they will plunder and burn, and all who are left alive will be carried off as slaves—slaves of the fierce and ignorant Ethiopians. But not I. For I would die first. I would not be carried off to be made a mock of, no, nor to be tortured so that I must pray the gods for a swift and easy death.'

'Why should he fail?' asked Humphrey shuddering.

'My father is wise and cunning and the Ethiopians are ignorant and foolish. And my father has devised a scheme whereby he may trap the enemy among the desert rocks—but—' He stopped speaking and looked at the children with sudden suspicion. 'Why should I speak to you of these things which no man knows, save I—'

'And those that betray you!' finished Peter quickly, remembering the old story.

The boy sat up, staring at them in amazement.

'Are you gods,' he asked at last, 'that you know the hidden secrets of men?'

'We are your friends,' said Peter softly, 'and we have come to help you!'

153

For a moment the young prince sat sunk in thought. At last he whispered, 'I will tell you what I would tell no man else. Early this morning I went to the temple to pray and I told no man of my going for I desired to be alone. It was so early that the stars had not yet failed, and I thought of my father wakeful beneath his tent.

'As I entered by my own private door, I saw the vizier and the high priest come together from the priest's inner room. Now that was sufficiently strange, since those two bear no love one to the other. Therefore I hid behind a great pillar and no man saw me in the shadow. And then I heard. Every word I heard. The Ethiopians had bribed them with gold—the very gold they have plundered from our caravans, and with the promise that those two should govern this land for their masters the Ethiopians. Therefore they are pledged, these two, to deliver my father and all the host of Egyptians with him, into the hand of the enemy.'

The boy hid his face in his hands.

'But what have they actually *done?*' asked Sheila.

'They have disclosed my father's plan, to lie in wait for the enemy and encircle them. The Ethiopians know the very spot where our armies lie, and they will come round and about the rocks and catch my father as a rat is caught in a trap.'

'Isn't there any way to warn him?' asked Sandy.

'There is no help save in the gods alone. But—' he struck his two hands together, 'if I could get to him—'

'If?' asked Peter gently.

'I would warn him, and he would change his plans. Maybe

154

he would lie in wait nearer their fortified place, maybe he would fall upon the armed camp by night. I do not know, for I am no general, I have too few years. But my father would know for he is very wise. But he is many days' journey hence, and no man save he be a god could reach him.'

'You shall reach him!' Peter said.

'Are you crazed?' asked Prince Usertsen. 'Or—' he gazed closely at Peter with eyes grown once more suspicious, 'do you seek to lure me hence and deliver me, also, into the hands of my enemies?'

Peter shook his head. 'We are your friends,' he said simply, 'and we will help you!'

Still the boy's steady gaze searched Peter's face. At last he said slowly: 'I do not understand the promise you have just made, for no man may help me.'

'Come and see for yourself!' Peter replied eagerly. 'You needn't go any farther than your own garden.'

'I believe, indeed, that you are my friends,' said Usertsen. 'Come let us go to Pharaoh's private garden.'

The children followed him through the vast hall, through long columned corridors and out into a fair garden. They looked neither to left nor right, though the flowers were bright and strange to the children, and fountains sprang to the sky, and bright-feathered birds sang sweetly in curious trees. Their feet went swiftly across the ground.

They followed Usertsen along a narrow, twisting path, until they stood in a green enclosure hedged about with thick-growing wistaria.

'Here we are safe!' said the prince.

Peter set his ship upon the ground.

'Tell me your father's name,' he said. 'We don't want any mistakes.'

'Amenemhat the First,' said the boy proudly. 'It is a good name of a good king.'

'Take us to the King Amenemhat the First!' cried Peter. The ship began to grow. The sails began to fill.

Usertsen stared as if he could no longer trust his eyes. He stepped forward and was about to touch the ship with his outstretched hand when he drew back.

'How do I know that there is not some evil spell here to destroy me utterly?' he asked. He stood for a moment in thought, then he fell with his face to the ground and prayed aloud. 'Osiris, Father of the gods, and Thoth in whom is all wisdom, give me now your good counsel.'

For a few moments he lay stretched upon the ground, then he rose to his feet and went close to Peter, looking him straight in the eyes.

'I will dare this thing,' he said, 'and more also. And if you betray me, may the gods deal justly with you when you come to the Hall of Judgement.'

And he stepped aboard.

The ship lifted gently into the air, and swiftly and smoothly it winged through the clear, bright sky. Usertsen stood with Peter at the prow, his eye set on the distance. 'Surely,' he was thinking to quieten his troubled heart, 'surely the gods are with me!' But frightened and troubled and amazed as he was, the young prince gave no sign, for he knew that a Pharaoh of Egypt must never betray fear by look

or gesture. So now he stood by the prow with Peter
motionless as a figure in bronze.

At last the ship began to drop, and soon the children could
see spread below them the tents of Pharaoh. Now and again
the sun would catch a burnished spear-head and set it
flashing white and dazzling in the sunlight.

When the ship had come safely to ground, they stepped
out and stood waiting for it to shrink again, and wondering
what they were to do next.

'Hadn't you better go first?' Humphrey suggested to the
prince. 'We'll follow!'

'It is well to prepare my father,' Usertsen answered, and he
set off rapidly. The children, following a little behind, could
see the astonishment of the soldiers as they turned to stare at
the figure of their prince. At last Usertsen reached the royal
tent.

Pharaoh was standing before the tent, talking to the
Captain of the Guard. The children knew at once which was
Pharaoh, by the golden cobra at his girdle and upon his head,
but more than anything they knew him by his proud and
royal bearing.

His hands lifted a little when he saw his son, but on his
face there was no sign of his great astonishment.

'How have you come hither,' he cried, 'across perilous
mountains and with so much speed? And why have you left
the land I entrusted to your hands?'

Usertsen knelt before his father.

'I came because I had to, there was no other way. They
have betrayed you, Neru Ammon the high priest and Nek-
Sekhet, in whom you put your trust. The enemy await you

157

in that very pass where you had planned to surprise them.'

'This is not possible!' cried Pharaoh. 'I am in the midst of a dream. These men are my friends proved and tried. They are upright men who would not betray their country into the hand of the enemy.'

'Yet it is true,' said Usertsen. 'For they hope to hold the land for the Ethiopians and to govern it in your stead.'

And he told Pharaoh all that he had that morning learned in the temple.

Then Pharaoh was seized with anger so that the veins in his neck stood out like whip-cord, but there was no other sign of his great wrath, for his face was smooth, and his voice, when he spoke, mild.

'This is no time for anger,' he said, 'nor for any talk of punishment. First we must fight. And when we return in victory, then I shall deal justly with the traitors.'

The children came forward and stood behind the prince, Peter still holding the magic ship in his hands.

Pharaoh turned abruptly at the entrance of his tent. 'Who are your companions?' he asked. 'And if it was but this very morning that you were in the temple, how did you reach this place which is many days' journey away?'

'I think these must be gods who have come to us at need,' said Usertsen slowly, 'and as for our journey, we came in that ship.' And he pointed at Peter's tiny boat.

Pharaoh looked steadfastly into the face of his son. 'Now I see in very truth that the gods have afflicted you with madness,' he said sadly. 'Come with me into the coolness of the tent. This madness, maybe, will pass away. Meanwhile,' he turned to the Captain of the Guard, 'keep these strangers fast, let them not out of your sight!'

The prince followed his father into the tent, his backward glance and beckoning finger invited the children to follow. They stepped in behind him, the captain smartly at their heels. Peter, ship in hand, bent to the floor.

'Now you shall rest,' began Pharaoh, but the words died away in his throat, for Pharaoh, Pharaoh who must never betray his innermost feelings, was staring, stiff with astonishment at the sight of the growing ship.

'I—I too—am afflicted,' he thought in horror. He looked at the Captain of the Guard and saw that he, too, was astounded by the miracle.

Peter bent again to his ship and whispered. The amazed Pharaoh saw it shrink and the sails roll themselves up. Once more it lay, tiny, on the palm of Peter's hand.

'This is some snare spread for us by Set the Wicked One, from whom Isis and Osiris shield us! I will not set foot upon it.'

'Then is our land lost and its people betrayed,' said Usertsen softly.

For a long moment there was silence. Then Pharaoh spoke. 'You are right, my son,' he said. And Pharaoh, the mighty, fell upon his face to ask counsel of the gods.

When he had made an end of praying, he rose to his feet and said, 'I will go with you.' Then he invited the children to be seated and he ordered his servants to bring them refreshments, the best that could be obtained. But he himself would take nothing, only he sat at a rough table, poring over a great map.

'See,' he said, and it was as if he talked to himself. 'Here are we. And this is the pass in which we planned to lie in wait. And here—' his finger moved farther on, 'is the stronghold of the enemy. If I could but reach it with fifty men and fall upon it by surprise, then the victory would be mine. But—' his hand fell to his side, 'their men would be on the march long before I could reach it, and it could not be done.'

Peter came forward quickly. 'Yes it could,' he cried. 'My ship will carry you and your men wherever you wish to go.'

'There is no ship in the world that could perform that task,' answered the king.

'Give your orders and I will carry you and your men wherever you wish to go,' said Peter eagerly. 'And,' he added, 'in time.'

Again Pharaoh seemed to meditate, his head on his breast.

'It is the gods who offer help,' said Usertsen softly.

Pharaoh lifted up his head and spoke. 'I trust in your word and thank you with all my heart.'

Soon bustle and noise told the children that the tents were being packed away and the beasts laden with baggage, and that all was being made ready for the march. The army was to take the road and meet Pharaoh and his picked band after the attack, together with the prisoners and the spoil.

It was nightfall when Pharaoh returned to the tent. Then his men put upon him his cuirass of bronze scales, and in one hand they put his great shield and in the other his tall spear; and about his waist they hung the leather belt with a short, sharp dagger, and upon his head they put the bright helmet with the royal serpent upon it, that all men might know and follow Pharaoh in the field.

Then Pharaoh and his son and the four children went out on to the flat space before the king's tent. It was quite dark and the inky-blue sky unpricked by any star, nor was there any moon. Only by the light of the flaring torches could they see the great army drawn up in order, the cohorts standing at attention, the generals and the captains each in his place.

All eyes were drawn upon the slight figure of the strange boy carrying a tiny ship in his hand.

The boy bent over and put the ship upon the ground. 'Take Pharaoh and his men to the stronghold of the Ethiopians,' he cried, and his voice went ringing to the furthermost men in the ranks.

The ship began to grow.

All eyes were fixed upon it in utter wonder. The foremost lines of men were forced to step backwards as it grew. Larger and larger grew the ship, and backwards, ever backwards moved the men.

At last Peter said, 'It is ready!' and the chosen band marched on board. Man after man, clad in the linen corselet of battle, each with his bow and spear and his battle-axe. When each man stood in his place, Pharaoh and his son and the four children stepped on board.

The sails swelled in the wind of their own making, the ship began to rise. On the prow with Peter stood Pharaoh looking like a man in a dream.

Swiftly and silently the ship cut its way through the night sky, nor on board was there any sound, for all were awed at the strange happening, so that it was like that Ship of the Dead which every man there believed would one day carry his soul to judgement.

Pharaoh turned to his son and whispered in the darkness, 'As soon as we are landed you must return to Lisht!'

Usertsen made a movement as if he would refuse, but Pharaoh said quickly and softly, 'This is your part to play. Too long already has Pharaoh's son been absent, and the prince missing. What better moment for the traitors to revolt? Hasten, and seize the traitors for me and cast them into prison. I will deal faithfully with them when I return.'

At last the ship began to drop and the watchers on board could see the darkness pricked by red watch-fires. Straight and swift and silent as a hawk the ship plunged downwards into the heart of the camp. When it lifted again into the air there arose shouts and confusion and the ring of steel upon steel.

The tiny points of red flowered suddenly into flame.

'My father has fired the camp!' cried Usertsen exulting. 'It is victory!'

He said no more but stood silent and still, his backward gaze fixed until the last glimmer of red had vanished in the darkness.

Swiftly and surely the magic ship winged through the dark night sky, and now, by the slackening of its speed, the children knew they had reached the city. The boat sank gently and settled upon firm earth, and the prince descended. Before them stood the huge dark bulk of the palace; the sweet fragrance of lilies came up to them in the darkness. And now Usertsen begged the children to descend and go back with him to await Pharaoh and the feasting and the sacrificing and the merry-making. But they shook their heads.

'It is time for us to go!' they said.

Then Usertsen knelt before them. 'I praise the high gods,' he said. 'And I will never forget this wonder. It shall be carved upon the pillars of the new temple my father shall raise in honour of this day. As for myself, I will sacrifice to the gods every day of my life! And so farewell!'

'Good-bye! Good-bye!' cried the children.

Peter put one arm round the neck of the golden boar. 'Home!' he whispered. And as the magic ship climbed into the air, the children at the prow gazed downwards until the kneeling figure became one with the darkness.

CHAPTER 12

Matilda Comes

It was Easter. Down by the brook the pussy-willow was out. In the ditches there were primroses for the plucking and the air was sweet with violets. The children were home again for the holidays. It was so lovely out in the fields and lanes where the hazels waved golden tassels and scarlet banners; it was so lovely down on the beach where the sea flashed like a mirror in the sunshine, and the wet pebbles winked with rays of light, that the children could never decide where they preferred to be. But at any rate they were content to put adventures on one side and race about, free as birds.

More than three months had gone by since the last adventure, but most of that had been spent at school; and what with football and hockey and acting and different societies—and lessons of course—there hadn't been much time to go adventuring.

It was at the beginning of the second week of the holidays that Peter, stretched lazily under a tree, suddenly realized that a whole precious week had somehow or other slipped away.

'What about another adventure?' he asked, sitting up suddenly and feeling that he couldn't bear to waste another minute.

'Too nice here!' Sheila said lazily.

'The trees smell like almond pudding!' added Sandy.

'Greedy little pig!' said Sheila sitting up.

'What's wrong with almond pudding?' asked Sandy in a very argufying voice.

'Nothing!' Peter answered kindly. 'Jolly nice! I wish I had some here!'

'It's not poetic,' Sheila explained. 'If you say the air smells like almond, that's poetry. If you say it smells like almond pudding, that's piggy!'

'I don't see it!' Sandy said obstinately. 'I think you're being simply horrid!'

'Shut up, you kids,' cried Peter. 'What will your visitor think if she hears you quarrelling like that?'

'I'm awfully excited about Marie!' Sheila declared, hugging her knees. 'Mother's a lamb to let me have her!'

'So she is!' Sandy agreed. 'I like Marie a lot. What time is she coming?'

'I don't know exactly. Some time this afternoon. Her luggage came yesterday. I helped Gertrude unpack. Marie's going to have the visitor's room. I put flowers there this morning and it looks lovely!'

'Well,' said Peter, not too pleased, 'if we're expecting a visitor we can't very well go off on an adventure now! I say,' he asked anxiously, 'I suppose this doesn't mean that we can't have any adventure all the time she's here? What sort of kid is she?'

'You'll soon see,' Sheila declared, 'but I'll just tell you this—She's my best friend at school and her home's in

Caen—that's Normandy, and she can't get home for these holidays. And though she's French, she can climb as high as any of us, and she can run a good deal faster. And she can keep a secret, too! And—'

It was at this moment that a telegraph boy came whistling up the lane. Peter got up to take the wire. It was addressed to Sheila.

'I expect it's from Marie,' she said tearing open the orange envelope and feeling very grown-up indeed. 'I should think it's to tell us just what train she's coming by!'

She was right. And she was wrong.

It was from Marie. But it was not to tell the time of her arrival. It was to say that she had developed measles and would be spending the rest of the holidays in the sick-room at school.

'Poor old Marie!' sighed Sheila, thinking first of her friend's disappointment. And then she thought of her own—of the visitor's bedroom and Marie's clothes neatly folded in the drawers, of Marie's frocks neatly hanging upon hangers, of Marie's vases gay with flowers, and her lips trembled.

The others, too, were feeling sad, for they had all looked forward to a new companion to share their fun.

Suddenly Humphrey sat up and began to smile. The others looked at him in annoyance, wondering why on earth he was smiling when they were all so disappointed. Then he went from bad to worse. Instead of just smiling, he began to laugh, and the others felt more annoyed than ever.

'Listen!' he cried, when he could manage to speak at last.

'Let's have our visitor after all. Her things are here. All we've got to do is go and get her.'

'But we can't!' explained Sheila, wondering whether he had suddenly gone off his head. 'She's got measles.'

'No she hasn't. Not my visitor,' replied Humphrey enjoying their looks of surprise. 'Remember Matilda? Remember we promised to go back for her? Well, let's go!'

'Jolly good idea!' cried Peter joyfully. 'We *did* promise, and it was rotten of us to forget her.'

'So it was,' Sheila agreed. 'She got us out of a tight corner.'

'I wonder if she got into trouble for it?' said Sandy thoughtfully.

'We never even bothered to find out!' Humphrey said in an ashamed sort of voice.

'Well, her old man wasn't too inviting, was he?' Peter demanded.

'We don't want to be thrown into that tower again,' said Sandy firmly.

'We needn't be. Now we know what to expect if we're not careful, we can *be* careful, can't we?' insisted Humphrey. 'Look here, let's go and get Matilda, now, this very minute!'

'Sound notion!' Peter agreed warmly.

'Just a minute,' Sheila said, sensible as ever, though her eyes were sparkling, 'this needs thinking over! Mother said I could have my friend—' She ticked the points off with her fingers. 'Well, that particular friend can't come because she's ill, so can we change her for another one? I suppose the answer is, *Ask mother!* But we can't ask mother since she and daddy are up in Scotland!'

167

'Fortunately!' grinned Peter. 'I'd like to know how you'd explain Matilda!'

'I don't think mother would mind,' Humphrey said.

'I don't think she would, either,' agreed Sandy.

'I suppose one person's as good as another!' said Sheila thoughtfully.

'Then we all agree?' asked Peter, looking round.

Three heads nodded.

'I'll just nip in and get the ship!' said Peter.

'I'll just nip in and get a piece of chocolate or a few biscuits,' said Sandy. 'It's a long way!'

'I'll just nip in and tell Gertrude that we shall be back with our visitor quite soon,' said Sheila.

Humphrey found himself alone in the garden. He walked up and down the path whistling with pleasure at the thought of seeing Matilda again. How on earth, he wondered, could they have forgotten her so long? There seemed no sign of the others returning, so he strolled into the house to hurry them up.

The playroom was empty, a cupboard door flung wide open, where Sandy had been rummaging for chocolate. He went over to close it, and stood for a moment looking down at his model engine on the bottom shelf.

Until the coming of the flying-ship it had been his pride and joy, but now he hardly ever thought about it. He felt a twinge of shame as he took it up in his hand. It was not above six inches in length, but it was quite, quite perfect. He poked his finger under the tiny boiler. Yes, there was a scrap of Meta fuel left.

How much longer would the others be?

At this moment a whistle from the garden made him jump. He thrust the engine into his pocket and raced downstairs.

'We've been waiting for you for *ages*!' said Sandy reproachfully.

'Well, I like that!' Humphrey exclaimed. 'I've been waiting for *you*!'

'Now children,' said Sheila in her most grown-up voice, 'don't quarrel. As a matter of fact I couldn't find Gertrude, so I had to hunt for her.'

'And I was hunting for Sheila,' Sandy explained.

'And I was hunting for both of them!' said Peter with a grin. 'Ready?'

The others nodded, and soon they were all running down the beach, and in a moment the boat lay on the smooth sand.

'To Matilda!' cried Peter. And so that there should be no mistake, added, 'And the time of William the Conqueror!'

Up rose the ship obedient to their wish. Now tree-tops and roofs of houses were left far below, and they saw the black cloud racing towards them up the sky. Humphrey leaned over in excitement, for here was the cloud—and behind the cloud, Matilda.

'I wonder what's really underneath that cloud?' asked Sandy. 'I mean, if we could look through it, what would we see?'

'The past. Spread out like a map,' Sheila answered.

Humphrey leaned over the side of the ship, trying to peer down through the blackness. As he did so, something fell from his pocket and he uttered a cry of dismay.

169

'There goes my engine,' he said. 'My special model one!'

'You chump!' said Peter. 'Whatever did you bring it for?'

'I don't know. It was in my hand when you whistled.'

'I wonder where it is now?' said Sheila thoughtfully.

'Somewhere in history,' said Sandy.

'But where?' asked Sheila dreamily. 'It might be lying about the streets in the reign of Elizabeth, or Charles, or James, or any one. I wonder what they'll make of it!'

'Who cares?' replied Humphrey gloomily. He was wishing with all his heart that his engine was safe in his pocket and not exciting the interest of Tudors or Stuarts.

'It's getting lighter!' cried Sandy who hated the dark cloud and was always the first to notice the return of light.

'Good!' cried Humphrey. And at the thought of seeing Matilda once more all grief for his lost engine vanished.

The boat began to sink.

'I think,' Peter said thoughtfully, 'we ought to be careful where we land, we're not exactly popular here.'

'Listen,' Sheila said, 'I don't think we all ought to go up to the castle. It's too dangerous. Some one would recognize us at once. Suppose we land half a mile up the coast, and one of us goes off to find Matilda?'

'Who's to go?' asked Peter.

'I think it ought to be Sandy or me. You see, even if we were found out, they wouldn't do much harm to us, because we're girls. But if they caught you or Huff, well, they might cut off your head without thinking twice about it!' And she shuddered.

'I wonder how we'd look coming back to 1939 without our heads,' grinned Peter.

'You wouldn't come back at all!' Sheila said slowly.

'I suppose not!' said Peter, and he wasn't grinning any more.

He leaned over to give his order to the golden boar and the ship sailed beyond the creek where Matilda lived and landed farther to the north.

It was quite, quite deserted. The sea rolled lazily on the white sand, just as it had done half an hour ago.

'Do you think anything has really happened this time?' asked Sandy anxiously.

'It *does* look though, if we turned and walked across the sand for a quarter of an hour, we'd find ourselves where we started from,' answered Sheila.

'So it did last time,' Humphrey reminded them. 'Besides, what about the black cloud? We've come through it!'

Peter stroked his boat affectionately, 'It never has let us down, and it never will.'

'Now,' said Sheila briskly, 'what are we going to do?'

'I don't like the idea of one of you girls going alone,' Peter said.

'Neither do I,' Humphrey agreed.

'It would be quite all right, really!' Sheila assured them eagerly. 'And I ought to go because I'm older.'

'Honestly, I don't like it!' said Peter in a worried voice.

'Why not? Girls are just as sensible as boys. There's no reason why I should get into trouble any more than you! And if I don't come back with Matilda quite soon, you'll know he's pushed me into the tower and you can come and rescue me.'

'Wouldn't you be afraid down there, all alone in the dark?' asked Sandy with wide eyes.

'No!' answered Sheila. And then added, 'Well, not very. You see I'd know you'd be coming along to rescue me!'

'All right!' agreed Peter, and Humphrey nodded.

Sheila climbed out of the ship, passing her hand over the golden head of the boar as she did so.

'We'll stay here,' Peter promised. 'And then if there's any trouble we'll be ready!'

'There won't be any trouble,' laughed Sheila, and ran lightly over the sand. But soon she began to tire; the long woollen gown she wore was heavy about her legs, and her leather shoes, coarse and heavy, chafed her bare heels, especially where the sand had slipped in, and was gritting against her flesh.

She stopped and took off her shoes and went on, carrying them in her hand.

In spite of the discomfort she was enjoying herself. This was the first adventure she had ever undertaken by herself. And what an adventure! Alone in a country stranger than Timbuctoo, with the prospect of a prison cell at the end of it.

Soon their own creek came into view and again she couldn't help thinking that it looked exactly as it had done when they came down from the house a little while ago. What had happened to their own house? Had it completely vanished? Or was it still standing there, with the lilac swaying in the wind, and Gertrude making the air noisy with the whine of the vacuum sweeper, and cook bending flushed above her oven? Was time like a curtain that hung between

172

Then and *Now?* And if you could find a chink, could you peep through? 'But what does it matter anyhow?' she thought. 'It's magic, and that explains everything.'

She went up the beach path and past the cabin of the couple to whom they had spoken last time. The same dog leaped on his chain and snarled, showing his teeth as she went by.

It was all familiar. Yet it was strange, too. She had the most delightful feeling of excitement mingled with fear as she went on.

The woman came to the cabin door and shouted after her. 'Are you bound for the castle?'

Sheila turned back. 'Yes,' she answered.

'Will you take these eggs which I am bound to deliver this day, and I will give you this fine apple for your pains? See, the basket is not heavy!'

'Willingly,' answered Sheila.

With the basket in one hand and the apple in the other, she trudged on.

The old dame had not spoken the exact truth, for the basket *was* heavy, and the apple was no great matter, being hard and green and sour. But in spite of that, Sheila was glad of the good excuse to get into the castle. Besides, she was sure no one would give her a moment's thought, as she trudged in, a peasant lass, with her basket on her arm.

She was right. She passed over the drawbridge and into the courtyard. A kitchen-boy hailed her as she stood not knowing where to go next. 'Late with the eggs, slowcoach!' he cried, and snatched the basket from her.

173

Sheila straightened her back and wiped her hot face with her long sleeve. Then she looked about her. There was no longer the same bustle and excitement. Maids moved slowly across the courtyard, and stayed to gossip with the men at the drawbridge.

'The master's away,' Sheila thought. 'I hope he is at any rate. Oh, I do hope he is!' And she came to the door of the tower that led up to Matilda's little room.

She felt a little frightened as she began to climb the spiral staircase. Perhaps the master of the castle was at home after all! Suppose she ran right into him when she entered Matilda's room? Suppose he threw her into the dungeon? Suppose he didn't care about her being a girl and cut off her head before Peter had a chance to rescue her?

She shivered a little as she stood alone on the dark stone staircase. For a moment she was minded to turn tail and run back as fast as she could to the others. Then she remembered that she herself had insisted upon coming—and coming alone. She lifted her long skirt and ran quickly up the stairs.

She reached the top panting, and stood outside the little tower room to regain her breath. Luck was with her, for she heard the sound of Matilda's voice singing a little song. She pushed open the heavy door and went inside.

Matilda looked up with a quick frown; she did not choose to be disturbed by any Saxon serving wench. Then she sprang to her feet and caught Sheila by the hand, drawing her to the middle of the tower-chamber.

'Oh, is it you?' she breathed. 'And are you real? Or are you a dream as I have half-thought?'

174

'Real enough!' laughed Sheila, and held out a brown hand.

'I had thought you were a dream, all of you. Or that you had gone away and quite forgotten me. And I do not know which thought I liked least. And now you are here at last! But—' she looked beyond Sheila and through the door, 'where are the others?'

'They are waiting for you down on the beach,' replied Sheila. 'We didn't dare to come, the four of us together, in case we should be recognized.'

Matilda nodded. 'That was wise.'

'Did you get into trouble when they found we'd escaped?' asked Sheila a little anxiously.

Matilda shook her head. 'I was asleep when my father came with the news, so how could I have known anything?' she asked with an innocent look. 'But indeed,' she added quickly, 'he did suspect me. And if he had been certain, he would have put me, too, in the tower dungeon. Though not for long I dare swear!'

'Where is he now?' Sheila asked still anxiously.

'He is away. He is in London delivering an account of his stewardship to the king. Twice a year he goes to London and he hates it. He likes the country best and this castle where he is master. When he goes, they rejoice, the men and the maids, and it is little they do all day but play in the courtyard.'

'You were singing, too!' Sheila reminded her slyly.

Matilda drew herself up proudly. 'I fear no man—least of all my father,' she said. 'And I sing when I please! But come now,' and she laid a hand on Sheila's sleeve, 'what shall I do now?'

175

'Join the others down on the beach,' Sheila answered promptly. 'We've come to take you back with us.'

'Back?' echoed Matilda.

'Of course! We're going to take you back with us in the flying-ship. You *do* want to come, don't you?'

'Of course!' Matilda said a little doubtfully. 'I suppose I do. But it will not be easy. You see, first I have to get out of the castle without being seen. And then I shall be missed; and that will be awkward when I return.' Matilda paced up and down, her long skirt brushing the rush strewn floor.

At last she cried, 'It is well! If you will wait here but a little, I will return, and then we will go away together.'

Sheila sat down on the low stool before the embroidery-frame. The work had progressed since her last visit and she examined it with interest.

The minutes passed slowly in the tower-room. Sheila lost interest in the tapestry and began to fidget. Then, with a sinking of the heart, she began to wonder whether Matilda had forgotten—or betrayed her.

That was nonsense! She tried to calm her fast-beating heart, for, in spite of her own danger, Matilda had proved herself their friend.

At last her straining ears caught the fall of feet mounting the stairs. The door swung open, and Matilda stood on the threshold.

'It is well!' she said. 'I have arranged all. And by great good luck the courtyard is empty. Go you first, and wait for me behind the trees that stand before the drawbridge.'

The two girls walked swiftly down the path that led to the beach.

'I think it is easier to get in than to get out of my father's castle,' said Matilda, 'for I was nearly caught by the returning guard as I slipped through!'

'I thought you were never coming,' confessed Sheila. 'Well, now we've really got you we'll have lots and lots of fun and bring you back safe and sound the minute you ask us to!'

By this time they were walking swiftly over the sand. Both girls held their long skirts up on their hands; they were panting a little with exertion, and neither had much breath to spare for asking or answering questions. As they drew near the creek where the magic boat lay hidden, three bare-legged figures came tearing to meet them.

'How odd they look!' exclaimed Matilda nervously. 'I have never seen any one dress in so strange a fashion!'

'Of course not!' Sheila explained kindly. 'They're wearing the sort of clothes every one wears in our time.'

Matilda drew her puzzled brows together, but she said nothing.

By this time the five children had met.

'You've been ages!' shouted Sandy.

'We've been worried to death about you!' cried Humphrey.

'We were just wondering whether we oughtn't to come after you,' Peter said.

Then they all started talking at once, asking and explaining and not listening either to answers or explanations, so that you might have thought it was a flock of starlings and not human children at all.

Still chattering at the tops of their voices, they came to the magic boat.

'Pass your hand over the boar's head!' cried Sandy. 'You've got to, before you get in!'

Obediently Matilda touched the golden head. The others climbed in after her. Matilda looked down, a little troubled, at the bare white knees under the blue serge skirt.

'Have I *got* to show my legs like this?' she asked doubtfully.

Sheila nodded. 'Don't worry!' she said. 'It's much more fun than trailing about in a skirt down to the ground. Why, you'd be falling on your nose in no time. Besides, you look awfully nice, really you do!' She turned to the others. 'Doesn't she?'

'Lovely!' Sandy agreed.

'Top-hole!' said Peter and Humphrey together.

'Doesn't it feel *nice*?' asked Sheila.

Matilda nodded. 'It's queer though. It's lovely, of course, being able to move my arms and legs as much as I want to, but I—I—well, I'm not used to it and I feel somehow undressed.'

'You'll soon get over that!' Sheila assured her. 'And now we ought to be getting back. It's getting on for tea-time.'

'What is tea-time?' Matilda asked.

Sandy looked at her wide-eyed and was about to explain, when Peter cried loudly, '*Home!*'

Matilda gave a little gasp of fear as the ship began to rise, but Humphrey caught hold of her arm and gave it a kind little squeeze.

'Look out for the black cloud!' Sandy warned her.

And as she spoke it came tearing down the sky. Matilda crouched in the boat, cold and a little frightened. But all the same the delightful spirit of adventure was upon her, and she knew that she would not have missed this for anything in the world.

'It's quite all right, really,' Peter explained. 'It's a bit bothersome sitting in the dark so long, just for the first time!'

'But you soon get used to it!' added Humphrey.

And then Sheila explained how the great black cloud stood between the past and the present.

'It's very simple, really,' she said. 'On one side, there's history—yesterday or a thousand years ago, it's all history, and it's all on one side of the cloud. And then, on the other side, it's to-day.'

Matilda couldn't help saying that she didn't think it *was* very simple, but she agreed with Humphrey that she would soon get used to the idea.

Light was beginning to seep in at the edges of the cloud, and soon the ship was winging downwards through the bright blue sky. When it had grounded, Peter jumped out and offered his hand to Matilda. 'Welcome!' he cried.

'Welcome!' echoed the others.

Matilda looked about her with puzzled eyes. 'But nothing has happened,' she protested. 'Everywhere it is the same! When I go up that path I shall find the hovels of the English pigs, and standing on the hill my father's castle, and—'

'I hope you don't mind me saying so,' Peter was very red in the face, 'but I don't think I'd talk about English pigs if I were you—you see we're all English now!'

179

'I'm not!' began Matilda stormily, but Sheila said quickly, 'Never mind, it doesn't matter really! Don't let's start by quarrelling!'

The matter was very soon forgotten, for as they approached the road, where the half-dozen houses stood, Matilda gave a cry of pleasure. 'Oh, it is pretty, pretty!' she exclaimed.

'What is?' asked Sheila, pleased at Matilda's pleasure.

The little girl waved her hand. She would have liked to explain how cosy the red-roofed house looked, with its gay curtains flying, and its red roofs and its red chimney-pots. After the great gaunt, grey stone castle it seemed so little and friendly and warm. She tried to explain about its smallness, but Sheila, a little hurt, said that theirs was the biggest house in the village, so Matilda thought she'd better stop trying.

As they went up the garden-path she gave a little cry of delight. Lilies she knew well enough, she had seen them often in the cloister garden of the monks, but pansies and the full bloomy tassels of the lilac she had never even dreamed of. She wanted to run all over the garden to touch and to smell, but the front door was open and Gertrude stood ready to welcome them.

Gertrude gave a sigh of relief when she saw them. 'We were downright worried, me and cook, about you meeting the train all by yourselves. But all's well that ends well, and if you'll take the young lady upstairs to wash her hands, you can have tea right away! *Chocolate cake!*' she whispered in Sandy's ear.

'Come along!' cried Sheila, and Matilda followed her upstairs, stopping to admire the carpet at every step.

But if the outside of the house and the flowering garden had been a surprise, the bath-room was wonderful beyond all words. She stood in the middle of the black-and-white floor, staring about her and not knowing what to do next.

Sheila turned on a tap and Matilda's eyes nearly popped out of her head. She stood staring as if she could not believe what she saw. Then she said in a whisper, 'You command the river and it flows! It comes obedient and quiet into your room! Oh,' and she looked earnestly into Sheila's face, 'is this witch-craft?'

Sheila laughed. 'It's all very simple!' she said. 'I'll show you the pipes and tank and everything afterwards. Come on, hurry up. I expect you're hungry. I know I am!'

Matilda advanced gingerly and put a finger under the tap. Then she leaped away with a cry. 'The devil himself is in your water, it flows burning hot into my hand!'

'Of course it does!' Sheila ran the cold tap. 'And it isn't the devil, really it isn't. I'll take you down and show you the furnace. Haven't you hot water in your house?'

'Sometimes.' Matilda nodded. 'It is heated on the fire. We carry it in pitchers. And when we use the bath-house we light a fire there, too. But we do not use it often, as you may imagine! Feast days. Or for great visitors. It is not necessary to boil one's self in order to be clean!'

Sheila found it difficult to reply to this, so she suggested they should go downstairs.

Matilda followed her down into the dining-room, and her face lit up with pleasure at the sight of the pretty table. The bread was whiter and finer than any she had ever seen. She tried some marmalade because she thought it was a lovely colour, and then made a little mouth.

'It's bitter because of the oranges,' Humphrey said.

Matilda looked blank.

'You've never seen an orange, have you?' said Peter. He went over to the sideboard and put one in her hands. She turned it over, delighting in its shape and colour and scent.

'What do you do with it?' she asked.

'Eat it!' Sandy said quickly, and Sheila said it would be better to wait till after tea.

Matilda took her piece of chocolate cake and turned it about in wonder. That, too, smelt good, and she took a bite. The rapturous expression on her face told the children that she shared their own opinion of it, and soon she was eating her second slice. Tea she refused entirely. This hot, curious-looking liquid did not attract her, and she drank some milk instead. She thought in her heart of hearts that the milk they had at home, frothing creamy in the wooden bucket, and warm from the cow, was better than this, but she was too polite to say so.

Sandy could not understand why oranges and bananas and chocolate and tea should be so strange to their visitor, and Humphrey explained that the countries where these things grow had not been discovered in Matilda's time. Sandy was sorry for Matilda who had never before tasted chocolate, and she promised herself that she would share all she had; which promise, by the way, was faithfully kept.

After tea they raced down to the beach and the four children introduced Matilda to cricket. She found the bat awkward at first, but she had a good eye, and she was swift on her feet, so very soon she was piling up runs with a speed that made even Peter stare.

Sooner than any one would have believed possible, it was supper-time. Gertrude came in to inquire what the young lady would be taking, and Matilda, before she replied, tasted some of Sandy's puffed rice, and Humphrey's lemonade, and Peter's raisins, and Sheila's hot chocolate. She decided that it was all so delicious that she would like some of each for her supper all the time she stayed with the Grants. Then, up to the bath-room they went, where Sheila obligingly explained all about pipes and taps and furnaces and the kitchen range, and soon Matilda was bravely turning on taps and turning them off again as if she had been used to them all her life.

Matilda thought that everything in the bath-room was delightful. In fact, she confided to Sheila, it was the very nicest place she had ever been in. She enjoyed the pleasant soap smelling of lavender and frothing so easily in soft, warm water, and the curious-tasting creamy stuff that came out of a tube on to a little brush that went into your mouth and gave you a delicious cold feeling in your tongue; but best of all she liked the thick warm towels that came out of the hot cupboard. She lay in the bath, wriggling her toes in the warm and scented water, and singing to herself a little song in old Norman French that went curiously with the chromium taps and the white-tiled walls.

The bedroom with its soft bed and silk eider-down enchanted her, so that she could not make up her mind which room she really liked best. Her bare toes went dancing up and down the soft carpet. 'I am used to stone floors and fur rugs; everything is large and clumsy in my home!' she said.

The pyjamas, neatly folded on the eider-down, made her laugh. There she stood, dancing on her bare toes and shaking with laughter.

'What do I do with these?' she asked.

'Put them on of course!' Sheila was surprised in her turn.

'You mean I must *clothe* myself when I get into my bed?'

'Well, you don't expect to go to bed naked, do you?' asked Sheila, thinking that Matilda was joking. But Matilda nodded.

'What else?' she said. 'I never in my life heard of putting clothes *on* when you go to bed!' Then, seeing that this was just what Sheila *did* expect, she sat down obediently on the carpet and put the pyjamas on. Then when Sheila had said 'Good night and sleep well,' and had gone away, Matilda knelt down and said a prayer and jumped into the soft, warm bed.

For a little while she lay awake wondering at all the extraordinary things that had happened to her to-day. 'It isn't true! I must be dreaming. Truly I am in my own sleeping-chamber up in the tower.' She touched the silken eider-down with the tip of her finger; then she reached up, and, feeling for the switch, flooded the room with light. She looked all round her, smiling happily. 'It *is* true!' she said softly to herself. 'Really and truly true!'

She switched off the light and curled herself up in the soft and fleecy bed, and fell fast asleep.

CHAPTER 13
Matilda Goes

She was awakened by the sound of laughter and opened her eyes to inquire somewhat fiercely who had dared to disturb the Lady Matilda's slumber.

Then she sat up and blinked.

Sheila and Sandy, fully dressed, were sitting on her bed; they both wore grey flannel shorts and grey jerseys. Matilda looked down at her own pyjama-striped arm and blinked again.

'Had a good night?' asked Sheila. Without waiting for an answer she went over to the chest of drawers and pulled out a pair of flannel shorts and a jersey exactly like her own. She threw them across to Matilda. 'Hurry up!' she cried. 'Breakfast! And then lots of fun!'

What marvellous things Matilda discovered during that first day with the Grant children! To begin with, there was that extraordinary fire that burned steadily and never consumed the log, a fire that had no smoke and no chimney, and was lit by pulling down a button in the wall. How the others laughed to see her rushing back into the house, crossing herself in alarm, at the sight of her first motor! But who could blame her? For it really did look fearsome rushing down the road, its hooter pipping madly, its headlights glaring in the darkness, and looking only too like those dragons that Old Nurse told her about up in the tower-room. And how she stared and stared when Peter switched the wireless on, and couldn't really believe her ears when the music swept through the room. And you should have seen her licking her first ice, laughing at the tingle of cold on her tongue, and then feeling to find out whether her tongue was really all there!

It was on the second morning of her visit that Matilda first caught sight of the church. It was a very old church, and the moment she saw it Matilda felt puzzled; she kept giving it quick bothered looks, she didn't know why. And when she had followed the others inside, she kept turning round in a worried sort of way. There was something about this place, something—She was sure she had been here before. She looked about her again. No, she had never seen this delicate stonework fretted like lace, nor the roses and laurel carved in the old dark wood with the little devils' heads peeping slyly through; nor had she seen the coloured saints in the green and golden windows. And yet, and yet it was all somehow familiar. Again her troubled eyes travelled about the golden gloom; they rested on the great rounded arches of stone. And then she knew! She knew whom she was expecting to come in at the high stone door. For she remembered her father, walking through the unfinished aisle, talking earnestly to the architect he had brought over from Caen to build this church for the Glory of God. Then there had been no fretted stone nor soft-coloured glass, and when the church was finished it had stood with the sunlight on its yellow stone, bare and golden and perfect.

'The old church always wants patching up,' Sandy explained when they stood once more out in the sunshine. 'If it isn't the tower, then it's the stained-glass windows. And if it isn't the windows, then it's the rood screen, and if it isn't the rood screen, well then it's something else! Cheaper to pull the old thing down and put a nice new one up instead!'

Matilda was very angry at that! She felt the temper bubbling up inside her. Pull down her father's church! The church that her father had planned and built and spent a good deal more on than he could really afford! Why, she remembered one Easter, every one had had to go without something because they were feeling so dreadfully poor. She herself had gone without a new fur-lined cloak though the weather was still keen and she had shivered in her bed!

She stood there so shaken with temper that she actually couldn't speak, which was a very good thing; for Humphrey came to the rescue, telling her how proud they were of their old Norman church and how people came for miles to see it, and that Sandy was too young to understand things properly. So Matilda quietened down, and then Sheila began to tell her about the bazaar.

Every year the vicar held a fête day in aid of the church repairs. There was always a bazaar where you could buy the most exciting things; and there were sports—with prizes—for every one. But of course not prizes for every one!

The children had been worried in case these exciting events would happen after Matilda had returned home. 'For, indeed, I must be home when my father returns from London!' she said firmly.

'Won't you be missed before that?' Sheila asked anxiously.

Matilda shook her head. 'I told my nurse that I should ride over to Aldeburgh to visit my cousin Clothilde, and indeed all was set for the visit. And then you came, and so I was tempted to make another visit instead!'

'But won't they miss you at Aldeburgh?' inquired Humphrey.

Matilda shook her head. 'They will think I have changed my mind. I have done so often before! It is nothing new! So long as I am there to welcome my father on his return from London, all will be well.'

'How long have we got then?' asked Peter.

Matilda began to calculate. 'It is difficult,' she said, 'and very confusing. Your calendar is not like ours, and I do not know how many days to allow!'

'Well, if you stay another ten days,' said Peter at last when five faces lifted from five sums each with a different answer, 'I should think that would be all right!'

It was the very next morning that Sheila came in waving a slip of pink paper. 'Hooray!' she cried. 'It's all right! Bazaar's on the seventh! We shall just get it in before Matilda goes!'

'Hooray!' cried the others, and the Lady Matilda shouted as loud as any.

Five heads clustered together over the pink slip.

'Let's look at the sports first!' said Peter.

'I'm going in for the wheelbarrow!' cried Sandy. 'Be my partner, Matilda!'

'I do not know what that is,' Matilda replied laughing, 'but I will very gladly be your partner.'

Sheila's finger moved down the list. 'Potato race, skipping race, running—80 yards, 100 yards, 200 yards, obstacle—' she read.

'Who's going to open the bazaar?' asked Humphrey.

'What exactly is a bazaar?' asked Matilda. 'I did not rightly understand when you explained before.'

So Sheila explained all over again. 'And the money you get for selling things at the stalls goes to the church,' she finished.

'And every one has something to give? You too?' inquired Matilda anxiously.

Sandy nodded. 'We always make one thing each in the Christmas holidays and then again at Easter. Sheila made a dish-cloth and a kettle-holder. I made a needle-case and a pen-wiper. Humphrey made two bowls out of clay; he painted them and fired them in the kitchen oven. They're awfully nice, and they didn't crack as they generally do when you fire them. Peter's made a toy signal and a wooden railway-station—he's awfully clever with his hands. He's painted them, too—I mean the signal and the station—not his hands! The vicar ordered them for Tony—that's his son. He's mad about trains, and the vicar's madder!'

'Oh dear!' sighed Matilda, who hadn't been listening to the end of this discourse. 'This is dreadful! It is simply dreadful!' And she sat down at the table with her head in her hands.

'What is?' asked Sheila, going over to her.

'I have nothing to give!' said Matilda, holding out her empty hands.

'Well, it doesn't matter,' said Sandy. 'After all you're a visitor, it isn't your church!'

'Oh, isn't it?' Matilda said quickly. 'Well, if you want to know, it's more mine than yours!'

The four children stared at her as if she had suddenly gone crazy.

'I didn't tell you at first because I was cross when Sandy said it ought to be pulled down. And then, when I wasn't cross any more, I forgot to tell you.'

'Tell us what?' cried the four children together.

'My father built it,' said Matilda very proudly.

Then in the silence that followed this astounding statement she explained.

'The earliest part of this church is Norman, you showed me that yourself in the guide-book! Of course it's Norman! My father is pious though he is a fighter. Good at fighting, good at praying, like all proper Normans. And of course, like all proper Normans, he built a church. So you see, I must give something to the bazaar!'

'Of course you must!' agreed Humphrey quickly. And the others nodded. They could see how dreadful it was for Matilda to have nothing to give.

There they sat, the five of them, asking themselves what she could possibly do.

Suddenly Sheila spoke. 'You're awfully clever with your needle. That first time we saw you, you were doing some sort of tapestry. Remember?'

'Oh that!' said Matilda, and shrugged her shoulders.

'Yes that!' Sheila assured her eagerly. 'You don't see work

like that anywhere to-day. Except what's left of course—from history-times I mean. People go to see the Bayeux tapestry from all over the world.'

'What's the Bayeux tapestry?' asked Matilda.

'The kind of work you were doing that day. The work at Bayeux was done by William the Conqueror's wife—your godmother. Why, you can find a picture of it in every history book!' And she rushed over to the bookcase and took out a book. 'Look!'

Matilda nodded without much interest. 'I saw her once, she was working on it. I was very little. She was a grand lady. Very tall. She did not smile much.'

'Well, couldn't you do a little bit of tapestry?' Sheila rushed on, not even stopping to ask questions about Queen Matilda, although any other time nothing would have satisfied her but the whole story.

'I suppose so,' Matilda said. 'But what for?'

Sheila stamped an impatient foot. 'Don't you *see*? That kind of needle-work is as rare as rare. Any one would buy it. And they'd be glad to pay for it, too! Old Mrs. Anderson of Kelby Hall would snap it up and never even ask the price.'

'Do you really mean that?' Matilda's eyes were wide with wonder. 'I could sell a piece of work like that for a great deal of money?'

Sheila nodded. 'Will you?' she asked.

Matilda's eyes shone. '*Will* I?' she answered.

'We can give you lots and lots of wool,' Sandy said. 'Mother's got a bagful. And so have cook and Gertrude. And so have me and Sheila.'

'Let's make a collection!' suggested Peter not stopping to correct her grammar.

Soon all the children were busy rummaging in drawers and cupboards. Cook came in with a great ball of scarlet wool that was left over after knitting knee-caps to keep her knees warm; Gertrude found one ball of emerald green, and one of turquoise blue. From the tangled depths of the playroom drawer came bright yellow and purple which Sandy had once fancied for her best doll. Matilda said all these gay colours were lovely, but she needed something dark too, and this set them off hunting again. Mother's work-basket supplied a huge ball of black darning-wool, a skein of dark grey left over from the boys' sweaters, and dark brown from father's golf stockings.

Matilda sat on the floor with all the treasure spread about her.

'It is curious,' she said. 'We have fewer colours.' She touched with careful fingers the bright rainbow on the floor. 'But our colours are not so bright. They are soft and gentle. But I think they will last better.'

'Won't these do?' Humphrey asked anxiously.

Matilda nodded. 'Very well!' she assured them. 'I shall make a pocket like we wear on our girdles at home. But first I shall need a strong piece of linen.'

'What about this?' And Sandy held out a somewhat crumpled handkerchief

Matilda shook her head. 'No,' she said. 'It is not heavy enough. It would not take the weight of the wool.'

'It's a pity we haven't a piece of real hand-woven linen,' said Sheila thoughtfully.

'But we have!' cried Sandy. 'Up in the trunk. You know, that old dressing-table runner Aunt Ellie made on her loom. Mother doesn't use it any more. Wait a tick, I'll get it!'

They heard her footsteps flying upstairs, and a moment later she dashed into the room waving a strip of heavy yellowish linen.

'The very thing!' cried Matilda joyfully. 'Now I can begin. But of course I must first think out my pattern.'

Sheila handed her a writing pad and some crayons. 'I shall miss this when I go home,' she said looking at the pad, 'there is no paper, and vellum is hard to come by. I draw my patterns upon a piece of stone.'

The children sat as quiet as mice while Matilda scribbled away. At last she cried, 'Finished!' and they crowded round to look.

Matilda had drawn the magic ship. There it was, its crimson sails coloured in against a turquoise sky with white fleecy clouds. The boar's head and the shields were there in bright yellow, and four—no—five figures were roughly sketched in.

'It will be outlined in black, so!' said Matilda thickening a line with her pencil. 'Now you can see!'

'It's wonderful!' breathed Sheila.

'There's me! There's me!' cried Sandy excitedly pointing to a tiny figure in purple.

'And me! And me! And me!' echoed the others.

'And me!' Matilda reminded them.

'It's a perfect day,' said Sheila, 'let's go down to the beach. Matilda can get on with her work and we can take it in turn to read aloud.'

193

Humphrey went off to interview Gertrude on the subject of tea out of doors, and soon they set out together, Matilda carrying cook's best work-bag.

All the afternoon Matilda sat stitching with bright wools upon a piece of linen. In and out went the needle, flashing like a tiny sword in the sunshine.

On and on went her tireless fingers, and by the time Gertrude was seen coming down the slope, a boar's head grinned out at them from the linen square. Matilda stuffed it quickly into her bag, for it was to be a surprise until it was finished; then they all settled down to the excellent tea cook had provided. As soon as they had finished, Matilda started once more on her needlework, and by the time they scrambled to their feet to go home to supper, a bright blue sky shone about the yellow head of the boar.

Day after day Matilda stitched at her work. The children said you could see it growing!

At last it was finished. The children, clustered about Matilda, could not stop admiring it. And they were right, for it was quite perfect. The bright little picture stood out strong and clear, each tiny stitch even and true.

'It'll fetch pounds, simply pounds,' declared Sheila.

'Let's take it down to the vicarage,' suggested Peter.

Matilda shook her head. 'Nobody must know where it has come from. It is my secret,' she declared. 'We must slip it through the vicarage door when it is dark!'

'I'm glad that's finished,' declared Humphrey. 'Now you can practise for the sack-race. After all, you've only got the rest of to-day.'

Matilda Goes

After supper the children walked down to the vicarage. There was a great bustle of people coming and going. While the others stopped to talk to the vicar, Matilda managed to slip the parcel unnoticed through the door. Every one was anxiously discussing the possibility of the next day being fine. The vicar looked up at the clear starry sky. 'It'll be a scorcher!' he promised.

And he was right. The children, jumping out of bed, looked up into a blue cloudless sky. Then they remembered—and their pleasure in the bright day lessened. For this evening Matilda must leave them.

After breakfast the five children strolled down to the parish room to see how the stalls were looking for the bazaar. They found the place in the state of wildest excitement. Pushing their way through the crowd, they saw the vicar's wife holding Matilda's pouch in her hand, and showing it very excitedly to a group of admiring friends.

'No one knows where it comes from!' she was saying. 'There wasn't a card or a note or anything!'

'The work's marvellous!' exclaimed another.

An elderly lady took it in her hands and turned it over carefully. 'If it weren't so bright and so new-looking,' she said, 'I'd say it was antique.'

'How old would you have said?' asked another.

The elderly lady laughed. 'If I told you *how* old, you'd think I was in my second childhood. Why, it reminds me of the Bayeux tapestry!'

'So it does!' said the vicar's wife. 'It's a simply marvellous reproduction. Look, the linen's hand-woven.'

'I'd like to buy it,' said the elderly lady, who was Mrs. Anderson. 'I'd give three pounds for it!'

'I'd buy it at that price too!' declared another lady.

'Well,' said the vicar's wife, 'we'll have to put it up to auction.'

Sheila nudged Matilda slyly and Matilda looked at her with starry eyes. The children danced home to lunch treading on air.

'I bet Matilda's pocket is the best thing there,' declared Sandy.

'I bet it is!' Sheila agreed. 'I wouldn't be surprised if it fetched six or even seven pounds!'

'Race you home!' cried Peter who was more interested in sports than in bazaars. 'Good practice for this afternoon!'

Down the road sped the five children. Soon Sheila, Humphrey, and Sandy were left hopelessly behind. They stopped running and stood in the road watching the other two. Peter and Matilda reached the garden gate at the same moment; they stood there laughing and panting.

'I hope Matilda wins something this afternoon,' Humphrey said, 'she's such a sport!'

'Yes, isn't she?' Sheila agreed.

'It'll be horrid when she goes,' Sandy said.

By this time they had all reached the gate and they trooped upstairs to wash their hands.

'I'm starving!' declared Matilda as the good smell of dinner floated upwards. She was silent for a moment. 'I wonder how I shall get used to doing without things—you know, the things that won't have been discovered. No potatoes,' she ticked them off on her fingers, 'no sugar, no cocoa, no bananas, no oranges—oh dear, it *will* seem dull!'

'No, it won't,' Humphrey hastened to reassure her; 'you'll have honey and apples and wine and mead—'

At this moment Gertrude rang the dinner-bell.

After dinner they all went upstairs to make themselves look smart for the afternoon. Presently Gertrude came upstairs for an inspection of hair and nails. In her hand she held a letter addressed to Sheila. It was from mother and father, sending their love and hoping that they were all well and that their little friend had settled down happily. Enclosed there was a postal order for twelve and six, half a crown for each child to spend at the bazaar, which, mother wrote, should be taking place just now.

'Hooray! Hooray!! Hooray!!!' cried the children, and Gertrude promised to take the postal order down to cook and give them each half a crown instead. A few minutes later, five very neat children, each with half a crown tucked safely away, strolled down to the field behind the parish room.

The whole village, in its best clothes, had gathered together. Bright coloured frocks, gay flags of all nations, green grass, blue sky, and the village band tootling away above the chatter and the laughter, gave them a pleasant feeling of excitement.

'I *hope* I shall win something!' Matilda whispered to Humphrey.

'I'm sure you will,' Humphrey whispered back, giving her hand a little squeeze. 'You run awfully well.'

'It's not that I want a *prize*,' Matilda explained. 'You see a prize wouldn't be much good to me. But I've never had a chance to run and jump, and I don't suppose I ever shall again; I want to show myself I can do that sort of thing as well as any one.'

'You can. And better than most!' Humphrey said comfortingly. 'Look out, we're beginning!'

The first half of the programme was devoted to the children so that they shouldn't get too tired waiting about in the sun. The whistle blew, and the competitors crowded about the starting-point. There were a good many of them, for visitors had come in from Radcliff and from the neighbouring villages.

The gun fired and away they went. Up went the tape.

The five children took their places along with the others. Matilda's heart beat in quick, hard thumps. She was so nervous standing there in her sack that when the signal for starting was given she promptly sat down in her sack, and before she managed to rise again to her feet the others were hobbling and jumping half-way down the course.

'Never mind,' whispered Humphrey coming round to her after the race. 'We didn't win anything, either. We didn't expect to, really. Eddy Jones won it. He always does. His father's the greengrocer so he can practise all the year round—I mean Eddy, not the old boy!'

Sandy distinguished herself in the egg-and-spoon race by dropping her egg, and picking it up with her fingers instead of with the spoon. And then, as if that was not enough, she ran with it, in her excitement, the egg held firmly beneath her thumb. Of course she was disqualified to the sound of hearty laughter. And when she realized what had happened she roared with laughter herself.

Then came the hundred yards race. Matilda stood toeing the line at the starting-point. 'Oh, please, *please*,' she was praying, 'it's my last day and I want to win. I *do* want to win!'

Off went the gun and off went the runners. Matilda and Peter moved steadily forward. Gradually all the others were left behind. It was going to be Matilda. Or Peter. No, Matilda! Or perhaps both. They were so evenly matched and were running so well that all eyes were upon them.

'Pet-er! Ma-*til*-da!' yelled the children encouraging both of them in turn.

Peter and Matilda ran steadily on. They could see the tape coming nearer. Out of the corner of her eye Matilda could see Peter's flushed face and determined mouth. She summoned up all her strength. She threw out a hand to the tape. She and Peter reached it together.

Matilda sank down panting on the grass. 'Well done, oh, well done!' cried Sheila thumping her on the back.

Sandy caught her by the hand to drag her from the grass, and all five went to the marquee for a glass of lemonade.

After that, Peter won the 220 yards race, and Sheila won the high-jump, but that was only because the others were so rotten, she said modestly. Humphrey won the obstacle, pushing his way under strawberry nets, dashing through paper-hoops, finding his five hidden potatoes, and jumping over hurdles with a grimly determined face that amused every one.

After that they went back to the refreshment tent and had

199

tea which consisted of buns and lemonade and ices. Peter looked at his programme. 'Only grown-up races now,' he said. 'Let's stroll along and see how the bazaar's getting on. We can come back for our prizes at the end.'

Once inside the parish room each child rushed round to see whether his or her own particular gift had been sold. When they met together in the middle of the hall after this reconnoitre, reports were good.

Sheila's dish-cloth and kettle-holder had been acquired by that admirer of her talents, Cook.

Sandy's pen-wiper had been purchased by the vicar, who thought, and very rightly, that it would add an air of distinction to his writing-desk. The needle-case, being miraculously unsold, Sandy bought it herself at half-price (which was a good bargain) as a present for mother.

Gertrude had bought one of Humphrey's bowls because she thought it would be useful for 'pins and things' and the local schoolmaster bought the other to show his class what a boy of their own age could produce. Peter's railway station and signal had long been ordered, so now there remained only Matilda's pouch to track down.

It didn't look as though it would need much detective-work to do that! Indeed, it looked as though there was going to be trouble over Matilda's gift.

Mrs. Anderson was determined to have it, and so was Mrs. Barr of Wenderby Hall. The other would-be purchasers had dropped out, realizing that their purses were not long enough for them to stand against these two determined bidders.

The children had arrived just in time for the auction. The

vicar was standing on the platform holding the pocket in his hand. Mrs. Anderson and Mrs. Barr were standing together, each with a grim and determined expression on her face. Stall-holders had deserted their half-empty stalls and every one was standing about silent and amused as the bidding started.

'What will you offer,' asked the vicar, smiling over his spectacles at every one, 'for this piece of truly exquisite work?'

Sheila pinched Matilda's hand in excitement at this praise, and Matilda pinched her back again.

'I start at three pounds,' continued the vicar. 'What offer at three pounds?'

'Guineas!' said Mrs. Anderson.

'Three pounds ten!' said Mrs. Barr in a louder voice.

'Four pounds!' cried Mrs. Anderson.

'Guineas!' cried Mrs. Barr still louder.

'Five pounds!' boomed Mrs. Anderson.

'Guineas!' shouted Mrs. Barr.

The children held their breath as the price crept upwards.

'Eight pounds!' almost screamed Mrs. Anderson.

'Guineas!' yelled Mrs. Barr who did not seem able to say anything else.

'Nine pounds!' shrieked Mrs. Anderson.

At twelve pounds Mrs. Anderson let her hands fall to her side and sat down.

'Guineas!' breathed Mrs. Barr suddenly faint, and sat down too.

'Any advance on twelve guineas?' asked the vicar hopefully. He looked at both ladies and, seeing no response, continued, 'Going—going—' He stopped and looked at Mrs. Anderson encouragingly, but she shook her head.

'Twelve guineas,' said the vicar and smiled all over his face. There was a good deal of clapping and then he made a little speech.

'Ladies and gentlemen,' he said, 'whoever the unknown and most generous donor of this gift may be,' and Matilda wriggled in excitement, 'he—or she—deserves our very deepest and heartfelt thanks. If my memory serves me, twelve pounds—I mean guineas—' and he bowed to Mrs. Barr amid hearty laughter, 'is the largest sum ever given for one article at any of our bazaars. And it is pleasant to know that those ladies who understand the art of fine needlework,' here he bowed to Mrs. Anderson, 'assure me that the purchaser as well as our church is fortunate.'

To the sound of renewed clapping the children pushed their way out into the fresh air.

'Well!' cried Sheila and hugged Matilda. Matilda's eyes were shining, she could not speak.

'Let's get back to the sports,' suggested Peter.

They arrived just as the mayor of Radcliff was about to give away the prizes. Matilda went to receive hers and walked back to the others clutching a new-minted florin in her hand. Suddenly she felt very tired. It had been a long day, and now it was nearly over—and her wonderful holiday, too.

She walked silent between the chattering children. This was their world, their own real world. But friendly and happy though it was, it wasn't her world. Hers was a world of cold stone castles and grim fighting; of hardship and courage. Of courage! She was suddenly impatient of this pleasant easy world of theirs, where life flowed so smoothly. She was so tired that it was almost as though she moved in a dream. Nothing seemed quite real any longer. She heard Peter's far-away voice offer Sandy sixpence of his prize-money, she heard Sheila and Humphrey also offer and wondered vaguely why she did not give Sandy her own florin since she would have no use for it.

As they passed the old church, dark against the sunset sky, Matilda said softly, 'I'd like to go inside just for a minute. I'd like to remember what it's going to look like!'

'We'll walk on slowly,' said Humphrey who guessed that she wanted to be alone.

Matilda slipped into the quiet of the old church. Darkness softened the edges of the old yellow stone, but through the coloured windows light came stealing in bands of red and gold and purple and green.

She looked up at the old Norman arches, half-hidden in the gloom, and whispered, 'I shall see you again!'

She looked up at the tattered silk banners that had been taken in far-off battles, and at the marble crusader sleeping, knee crossed, in the dusk, and she whispered, 'But you I shall not see again!'

She turned softly and went out. Only by the door she stopped for a second. On the table stood a box labelled, *For the Upkeep of this Ancient Church.* From her pocket she drew the shining florin and dropped it into the box. She smiled a little as she heard it drop, then she ran out of the door and down the road into the evening sunlight.

Supper was a silent meal. Even Sandy pushed a half-empty plate away and said she didn't feel hungry any more.

'Too many ices!' said Peter gloomily, but he looked as if he didn't quite believe it.

At last it was time to go. Peter put his boat in his pocket and the children followed him down to the beach. There, in the fast-gathering dusk, he set the boat on the wet sand. Her face hidden as she shook her hair about her shoulders, Matilda replaited it neatly, swinging a dark braid of hair over each shoulder.

When all was ready, she stepped gravely into the boat, passing her hand over the boar's glowing head. Her long woollen gown swept the boards at the bottom of the boat, and she lifted it high in a small jewelled hand.

The others followed in silence.

'Back to Matilda's home!' said Peter in a low voice, and the ship heard and obeyed.

They sat there in utter silence, Matilda with her head bowed on her knee, the others gazing their last at their friend. They hardly noticed the dark cloud, so dark was the night. It was only when they saw the stars pricking through the sky that they realized that once more they were on the other side of time.

The ship flew low and stopped upon the sandy beach. To the left the path ran up—to Matilda's great stone castle, or to the little warm house from which the children had run a few minutes before? They were not at all sure, for they were weary and a little confused.

Humphrey climbed out and in silence offered a hand to the Lady Matilda. She stepped out gravely, her little chin held high, but Humphrey could have sworn that her eyes were bright with tears she would not shed.

'Good-bye, good-bye, darling!' cried Sandy.

'We shall come back for you!' Sheila promised.

Matilda faced them in the starlight. 'No,' she said very gently. 'I must live my own life in my own way and in my own time.'

Sheila and Sandy bent over quickly and kissed her.

'Good-bye!' said Peter gruffly and held out his hand.

Humphrey walked with her a little way over the dark ribbed sand.

'Good-bye, Matilda,' he said.

'I will never forget you,' she said steadily.

Humphrey said, 'I don't suppose I shall forget you, either!' They stood for a little while staring into each other's face in the darkness, then he bent forward suddenly and kissed her. He watched her pick up her long gown and, with head held high, walk steadily away up the path.

He stood there, watching until she was lost to sight, then he sighed a little and turned back to the others. It was only when they waved to him that he found himself wondering why he had kissed Matilda, he, who didn't believe in kissing. He hoped that the others had not seen him.

'Home!' cried Peter, and, as the ship rose again into the air, each child was thinking of Matilda who was their friend and wondering whether they would ever see her again. They dropped through the black cloud without even noticing it.

Their tired feet took them stumbling over the sand. They were half-asleep as they came up the dark garden path and into the bright, quiet room.

CHAPTER 14

The Specially Exciting Adventure

It was a summer again, and a whole year since Peter had fallen in love with a little ship in a dark old window.

The children were supposed to be in bed, but it was far too hot to sleep, so they sat on Peter's bed in the moonlight, talking softly. From the garden came the scent of the lime-tree—sweeter, Sandy said, than the dearest scent mother put on her handkerchief when she went to a party. Above the whispered talk they could hear the soft beat of the sea as it broke upon the beach.

The scent of the lime and the sound of the sea in the moonlight are exciting things to happen together—especially if you are not sleepy.

'It's no good trying to go to sleep,' Humphrey said suddenly. 'What about another adventure?'

'Do let's!' Sheila agreed quickly. 'We've had a lazy sort of day, and now I feel I'd like to do something.'

'So should I!' exclaimed Peter.

'Me, too!' piped Sandy.

'Any suggestions where to go?' asked Peter.

The children thought in silence.

'I know!' cried Humphrey after a while. 'Let's go back and find my model engine!'

'What on earth are you talking about?' demanded Peter.

'I dropped it through the time-cloud when we went to fetch Matilda, remember? It's fallen somewhere in history. It would be fun to see where. Besides—I'd like my engine back, it's a jolly good one!'

'Every one agree?' asked Peter.

All heads nodded together.

'What's the time?' asked Sandy.

'Quarter to ten,' Peter answered, glancing at his watch in the moonlight.

'It must be getting late,' Humphrey said after what seemed a very long while. 'There goes the clock.'

'One, two, three . . . ' counted Sheila.

'Four, five, six . . . ' continued Peter.

'Seven, eight, nine, *ten*!' finished Humphrey.

'Only ten!' exclaimed Peter.

'I thought it was midnight at least,' said Sandy yawning.

It seemed hours to them before the quarter struck and then the half.

'Let's wait another quarter of an hour,' suggested Peter.

After another tiresome wait they heard the clock chime the three quarters; Peter bent down and gently set the ship on the floor. 'Back to the time when Humphrey lost his engine,' he whispered.

In silence they watched the ship begin to grow. One by one they stepped inside. Then straight as an arrow the ship darted through the open window and up into the starry spring sky.

'There's the black cloud!' cried Peter.

The children sat impatiently through the darkness, wondering how long it would last.

'This ought to be a specially exciting adventure, because we don't know where we're going,' observed Sandy, trying to cheer herself up, for she hated the black cloud.

'Well, let's hope it won't be *too* exciting!' said Humphrey.

Gradually the cloud thinned and the clear stars shone through.

'Not such a thick cloud this time,' observed Peter.

'Then we're not as far back as Matilda,' said Sandy.

'Elizabeth perhaps,' suggested Sheila, who admired the Elizabethans passionately.

'Or Charles, or James, or Anne, or the Georges,' added Humphrey.

Down, down, down went the ship.

A faint pink came up over the sky. 'We're going down into the morning,' said Sheila.

'We've been out all night,' said Sandy happily.

The boat began to slacken speed. The earth grey with dew rose to meet them.

Humphrey jumped lightly on to the grass, touching the boar's head with his left hand. The others followed, and there they stood in the dewy grass staring at each other and wondering into what patch of history they had dropped.

'Give it up!' said Peter at last, pulling at his long, red hose and twisting about to get a good look at his short tunic. Sandy smoothed her long skirt over her hips. 'I wish I had come into history as a boy,' she said. 'I do *hate* these long skirts.'

Humphrey and Sheila were staring at each other.

'What date would you say?' she asked at last.

'Don't know,' he answered. 'Middle Ages I should think!'

'Can't be!' Sandy decided, 'because I don't feel middle-aged.'

When they had all finished laughing, they began to consider the question again.

'Can't we tell by the clothes?' asked Sheila.

'Not really,' Humphrey answered. 'Clothes didn't change a lot. Anyhow, as Sandy says, not Norman!'

'How do you know?' Peter asked.

'Because I dropped my engine *before* we got to Matilda. The cloud hadn't begun to thin.'

Presently, with a great burst of light, the sun came through, and it seemed as if all the birds in the world started singing at once.

'Well, it's Old England, anyhow, and that ought to be good enough for any one!' said Sheila, stooping to pick a buttercup. She thrust it through the blue lacing of her brown stuff bodice.

'Come on, let's find out where we are!' urged Peter, putting his ship carefully in the pouch that hung at his leather belt.

Over the wet grass they went, the long skirts of the girls brushing it green as they walked. The ground began to rise and soon they were climbing a high hill. Peter and Humphrey had to stop more than once to give a hand to the girls, who found it hard work climbing in their long, heavy skirts.

At last they reached the top of the hill and looked about

them. A broad and peaceful river, grey in the early morning light, wound gently before them. In the distance they could see a four-square tower standing high upon a hill and set about with strong walls. It cast a watchful eye upon the river flowing at its foot, as it stood sturdy and somewhat grim, protecting the town that lay behind it. The children knew there must be a town there in spite of the high walls that hid the houses, because of the smoke rising from the countless chimneys, for early as it was folk were astir. To the north, thickly wooded country stretched away to the sky.

'I wonder what that town can be!' said Humphrey.

'Let's go and find out,' suggested Peter.

The two little girls swung the tails of their long gowns over their arms and they set off.

It was pleasant walking through the flowering country-side. It was still very early, but the smoke was curling from the cottage chimneys as they went past. There came to their ears the pleasant country sounds—jingle of harness as the slow oxen moved, drawing the plough; the ring of axe upon wood. Country-folk gave them God Speed, and they returned the greeting with all their hearts.

Presently the girls in their long, heavy skirts could walk no longer. The boys, too, were glad to sit in the shade of a great oak-tree and take a breathing-space.

'I wish we could get a lift,' said Sheila, easing her shoe with her finger.

'I'm hungry,' Sandy said dolefully.

Peter put his hand in his pocket. 'Goodness!' he exclaimed, and drew out a coin. It was strange to the children, who stared curiously at it.

'I should think that's a silver penny,' said Humphrey after a little while. 'Let's have a look at it, I expect it'll give us some idea of what time we're in!'

But Peter had already turned it over.

'Rex . . . R-i-c-a-r-d-u-s . . . ' he spelled out slowly. 'That's Richard, of course!'

'First or Second?' asked Humphrey excitedly.

'Can't see,' replied Peter. 'It's too rubbed.'

'I hope it's the crusading one!' cried Sheila breathlessly.

'I expect we'll find out soon,' said Peter, 'and anyhow they're both thrilling!'

'How much do you think the money's worth?' asked the ever-practical Sandy.

'Don't know,' replied Peter. 'But enough to buy us some bread and cheese, I should think!'

'Listen!' cried Sheila suddenly.

To their ears came the far-off but quite unmistakable clip-clop of hoofs. The sound grew louder and louder.

It was a rich and important procession, with outriders and servants before and behind. In the middle rode a man with a tired and gentle face. He was clothed richly in scarlet and a jewelled cross flashed from his breast. His sleeves of white lawn billowed out from under his magnificent cloak, and he wore a broad-brimmed hat to protect him from the sun.

And now another party was seen coming towards them from the direction of the town. A heavy man rode at the head. He was clad in a long gown of sober stuff edged with rich fur. A heavy gold chain gleamed about his neck, flashing and glittering in the sunlight. His narrow eyes looked haughtily above his large nose, and his mouth was thin-lipped, although now it was doing its best to smile a welcome.

The two processions met in the middle of the road, just by the tree where the children were resting.

The man with the gold chain dismounted clumsily and stood with his bared head bowed in greeting. Suddenly, from the corner of his eye, he caught sight of the children sitting beneath the tree. He whipped round immediately. 'Rogues and vagabonds,' came his cold and angry voice, 'do you dare to be seated before the Lord Bishop?'

The children scrambled to their feet, and Peter opened his mouth to explain. But the other would have none of it.

'If you loiter about the country-side,' he broke in impatiently, 'I will have you whipped soundly, ay, and stood in the stocks!'

'The children meant no harm, Sir Sheriff,' said the man in the red cloak, and he smiled kindly out of his tired eyes.

'They are a plague and a pest upon the country-side,' said the sheriff bitterly. 'And who encourages them but that villain in the greenwood! Robbing worthy folk to pour their hard-won silver into the bottomless pockets of thieves and rogues like himself! If I could catch that wretch I would hang him high enough, I warrant you!'

'Peace, Sir Sheriff!' commanded the other, and his voice, low and gentle enough, allowed of no argument. 'There is business enough for to-day, and my heart is sore already. I think that you and the Prior of Lenton are altogether too zealous in this matter.'

In silence the sheriff mounted his horse and turned it about, and the two processions rode together towards the town.

'Did you hear that?' gasped Humphrey. '*The villain in the greenwood!*'

'Who robs the rich,' continued Sheila.

'To give to the poor,' finished Sandy.

Peter clapped his hands softly together. 'Robin Hood!' he cried.

'And the fellow with the gold chain was the sheriff of Nottingham!'

'And the man with the cross was the Bishop of—Hereford—I expect,' said Sheila.

'I don't think so,' said Sandy, who knew her Robin Hood book almost by heart, 'the Bishop of Hereford hated Robin, and that man didn't sound as if he hated any one!'

'Well, anyhow, whoever he is,' said Humphrey, 'that tower is Nottingham Castle, and those woods are Sherwood Forest.'

'And that settles which Richard it is. It's Lion-Heart—unless of course he's dead.'

'Then it would be John. I *hate* John,' Peter said with feeling. 'I don't want to come into his reign at all.'

'Well, it looks a good adventure!' said Sheila, and the others agreed.

The day was fine and the birds sang, and a cool wind had sprung up and was rustling like a sea in the leaves of the trees. A small, clear stream babbled away over shining stones, and the children stopped to drink. The boys pulled off their long tight hose and the girls kicked the shoes from their bare feet and paddled in the icy water. When they had dried their feet on the sun-warmed grass, they were well rested, and eager to finish their journey.

Now the road was growing more and more crowded, and several times the children had to back into a ditch for some wagon piled high with country produce and already late for market, or for a cart a-blossom with stout country wives and pretty maids all agog for the day's pleasure.

But now they saw the wall of the city right in front of them, casting a wide shade across the dazzling road. The great gates stood open, and along with the eager crowd they passed inside.

They found themselves in a narrow street overhung with houses; it was dark and cool as a tunnel after the open country. Soon the dark street led into an open market-square, and the children stopped, bewildered by the noise. Geese hissed, ducks quacked, and pigs grunted; cartwheels rumbled, pots and pans clanged, people talked, shouted, sang, and, like the creatures, hissed, quacked, and grunted.

Peter shouldered his way through the crowd and the others followed at his heels. They found themselves by a row of stalls. All sorts of cheeses were stacked up—great yellow cheeses, blue-veined cheeses, and small cream cheeses wrapped in muslin. Peter put his hand in his pocket for his silver penny. He bought a great wedge of famous Derby cheese, and handed over the money.

The man took it and turned it about, as if to assure himself that it was good, then drawing from his pouch some small silver coins he handed three of them to Peter.

215

'Here be three farthings!' he said.

'I've never heard of silver farthings before,' whispered Sandy.

'Neither have I,' Humphrey whispered back. 'I expect there aren't any coppers.' He looked at the great hunk of cheese in Peter's hand. 'A farthing buys a lot, anyhow!'

They strolled over to a stall in the next avenue, and with another silver farthing Peter bought a loaf. The bread was brown and coarse but very fresh, and to the hungry children delicious.

The woman who had sold them the bread was inclined to be chatty. She stood with her hands on her broad hips, smiling at the crowds surging along.

'We look to do good trade, to-day,' she said, 'for, indeed, it is busier than a holiday, or Goose Fair. Were you ever at Goose Fair? It is a fine sight for business or for pleasure—which you will! But to-day is better even than Goose Fair.'

The children looked at her eagerly and she went on. 'There is a man to be burnt this day. All right folk must rejoice, for he that is to burn is a witch!'

'There's no such thing!' cried Sandy scornfully.

The woman clapped a great hand over the little girl's mouth. 'Guard your tongue, child,' she whispered quickly.

'But—' began Sandy. Peter trod hard on her foot. 'Your pardon, Dame,' he said, 'but we are just from the country, my sisters and I, and we know nothing.'

'Those that know nothing had best keep a silent tongue,' said the woman tartly.

'Why are they going to burn him?' asked Sheila, her cheeks pale. 'What has he done?'

'Witchcraft. Suspected *and* proven!' answered the woman with satisfaction.

'Nothing is proven,' interrupted a man strolling over from the next booth and munching at one of his own honey-cakes. 'Except that he be one of Robin's men. If he were not wearing the forester's green, I doubt if my Lord Bishop of Hereford himself could push him an inch nearer the fire!'

'You and your Robin!' cried the woman scornfully. 'Not but what he isn't a rare fine fellow, and worth all the fat bishops in creation, ay, and Richard himself, though he be our crowned king! But what use a crowned king who goes gallivanting off to Jerusalem, leaving that brother John of his to bleed us dry with his borrowings and his taxings? Still, Robin or no Robin, I know what I know. The man is rightly to die. Even my Lord Bishop of Lincoln, who has no stomach for witch-hunting, has condemned him.'

'*What* do you know?' asked the man scornfully, taking another bite out of his honey-cake.

'Look you,' said the woman, 'what I tell you is true. The prisoner says he will make a wagon to go without any beast to draw it. And if not drawn by horses or by oxen, who then will move it? For never has any man seen a cart to go without any creature at all to draw it, no, nor ever will, though he live to the age of Methuselah!'

'This is not witchcraft,' said the man still scornfully, 'but rather madness—'

'But you have not heard the whole of it,' answered the

217

woman earnestly, 'no, not by half! For, indeed, he has himself made such a wagon!'

'*What* do you say?' inquired the man as though he dare not believe his own ears.

'Ay!' the woman nodded. 'I speak what I know. My sister, if it please you, is own servant to the sheriff.'

The man nodded.

'She heard him tell his lady. A small wagon of green, he said, and not above a hand's length in size, very curiously fashioned, being as round as a candle in the body. And the wheels not of wood, but of iron, as is the body also. And—you may believe me, for I speak no lie—there is a chimney from which the devil himself comes in the form of a hot cloud.'

She paused for breath.

'He did not fashion this wagon himself, he said, having picked it up in a field. A likely story, say I. And so said the sheriff. And his lady also. And so said my sister, she being crouched upon the floor, fastening her lady's shoon!'

Humphrey caught at Peter's sleeve. 'We've got to get out of this,' he whispered. 'Now, this minute!'

They pushed their way out with difficulty, for the crowd had grown even larger. Men and women stood about four or five deep, watching with eager eyes the dreadful preparations. Right in the middle of the market-place a wooden platform had been set up, and on it men were busily heaping faggots. The crowd in high holiday humour were offering advice.

'More wood there!' cried one.

'And see that it be not green!' cried another.

'Be not careful with the pitch,' came from a third.

'I do love a good blaze,' chuckled another, who could hardly speak for laughter.

Humphrey was fighting his way out with his fists.

'Hurry, oh hurry,' he cried breathlessly to Peter.

At last they were through the gate, but the road was still blocked with people swarming in to see the fun. Peter pushed his way through a hedge, and there, in an open field, with no one but sheep to observe him, drew out his ship.

'Where to?' he asked.

'Robin Hood,' answered Humphrey. 'Oh, will he be able to do anything, anything at all!'

Soon the children were flying swiftly through the air. 'Now,' demanded Peter, turning to his brother, 'what's it all about?'

'It's my fault,' Humphrey said miserably.

The others stared as if he had suddenly taken leave of his senses, but he went on. 'You remember I dropped my model engine through the time-cloud? Well, this chap must have picked it up, and, being a bright lad, he put two and two together and they made four. I mean he made the model work. No one else can understand it. Of course they can't. So he's going to be burnt. And it's all my fault!'

He turned his head away so that the others shouldn't see that he was almost crying.

Sheila put out a hand. 'It's not your fault—it isn't really. You weren't to know. I mean how could you?'

'Shall we ever get there?' asked Humphrey.

219

'We're there already,' cried Sheila. 'Look, we're beginning to sink!'

Sure enough the ship was sinking steadily, and in less than five minutes they were standing on a sandy common thickly set about with trees.

CHAPTER 15

Dickon

They had not gone above a hundred paces before the cry 'Halt!' rang through the wood. A tall man in green, his thin face like carved wood, stood before them, barring the way.

'Oh, don't stop us, please!' Humphrey begged. 'We've *got* to find Robin Hood!'

The man with the brown face said grimly, 'No man sees Robin Hood, unless Robin Hood desires to see *him*!'

'We're not bishops or abbots or anything like that!' Sandy explained.

Peter spoke, in a surprising tone of authority. 'While we waste words, your comrade may burn!'

'We are from Nottingham,' added Humphrey gravely.

The man stood staring at them for a full minute. Then, 'Follow me,' he said. 'And if you have deceived me, God pity you!'

Robin was sitting beneath his favourite oak, tightening the string of his long-bow. He stared in amazement at the little party coming towards him through the trees.

'God's body!' he swore. 'Has my greenwood become a nursery?'

Humphrey came stumbling forward. 'Robin Hood,' he cried, 'your man is taken in Nottingham, and they are going to burn him!'

'Which man?' asked Robin with quick suspicion, for might not this be yet another trick on the part of the sheriff to lure him into the city. 'And why have they taken him?'

'They have taken him for witchcraft,' cried Humphrey.

'Because he said he could make a wagon go without any animal to draw it,' added Sheila.

'And when they took him he had in his hand a tiny wagon—though it was nothing but a toy,' Humphrey continued miserably.

'How do you know all this?' asked Robin, looking keenly into one young face after another.

'It's true, honestly it is! Every word of it!' Humphrey said imploringly. 'Do come with us!' And he caught at Robin's green sleeve.

Robin stood trying to make up his mind. Was this indeed the truth they were speaking?

'Listen,' said Peter. 'You doubt us. And you are right to doubt, because you might pay for trusting us with your life. But if you'll come with us, I'll leave my sisters behind to show we are telling the truth!'

Robin pulled at his beard. 'If you will leave the two maids,' he said at last, 'I will come with you!'

Sandy opened her mouth to object, but Sheila said quickly, 'This is part of the adventure. *Our* part!' And Sandy nodded.

Robin turned to the dark-faced fellow in green. 'Conduct these damsels to Maid Marian,' he ordered, and Sheila and Sandy followed their guide deep into the heart of the greenwood.

Robin Hood strode backwards and forwards, muttering in his beard as he rejected one plan after another. Humphrey followed him with his eyes, imploring him to think quickly.

'They were heaping the faggots for the burning when you left the city?' Robin asked at last.

Humphrey nodded.

'Then what can I do?' asked Robin, lifting his hands and letting them fall again in despair. 'That will be all of three hours ago. If we should fly with the wings of angels, my man is already sped.'

Peter said quietly, 'It's only a few moments since we left Nottingham, and in a few moments more we can be back again.'

Robin threw back his head and laughed. 'Then is the whole tale a jest—and there is no man of mine taken. You have tricked Robin right well!'

Peter said nothing. He bent down and set his little ship on the ground. 'Nottingham!' he cried.

Robin looked on curiously. What trick was this strange lad up to now? Then he stood staring, his eyes almost starting from his head.

'This is madness!' he whispered, and went on staring at the growing ship. 'Madness or witchcraft!' He crossed himself. 'I will have naught to do with it!'

'There's nothing wrong, indeed there isn't!' cried Peter. 'You've got my sisters, you know!'

'And while we waste words,' said Humphrey fiercely, 'your man may burn!'

'That is God's truth!' cried Robin, and he blew a sudden

223

piercing blast upon his horn. A forester in Lincoln green stood before him. So suddenly and so silently had he slipped from the shadows of the greenwood, that to the children it savoured of yet more magic.

'The habit of a travelling friar!' ordered Robin.

In a short while the man returned carrying a black garment over his arm. Robin drew the loose black gown over his green habit and tied it firmly about the waist with a rope. Then he drew the hood over his face so that only his fierce eyes showed.

'Witchcraft, witchcraft!' he muttered once more and crossed himself again. Then seeing that none of them shrank from the holy sign, he followed them into the magic boat.

The great sail filled. The boat sped swift as an eagle through the air.

At first Robin was too dumbfounded to think clearly, but soon the thought of his man in danger put all other ideas out of his head; he sat there, a hand pulling impatiently at his beard. Round and round went his thoughts. More than once, his plan almost complete, he would discover some detail that would endanger the whole thing. At last, as the ship sank upon the grass, he stood up in triumph.

'Now listen well,' commanded Robin, when they stood once more upon firm ground, 'and see that you understand your part, for upon it hangs all our lives.' He turned to Peter. 'You must make your way with all speed to the castle rock and take your stand upon the highest place, that is to the left hand as you face the river. There you must stand with the ship ready to hand, awaiting the signal. And having received the signal, you must delay not a second.'

'You,' he turned to Humphrey, 'shall give the signal. You must press close to the stake as you dare. When you see the priest stand upon the platform with the prisoner by him, you shall wave your cap in your right hand, thrice. Thus!' He waved his own hand slowly about his head. 'The signal must be plain to him who watches.'

'When you see the signal of the thrice-waved cap,' he swung back to Peter, 'you must command the ship to take you to the market-place, where you must dart down at your greatest speed and take up the prisoner—and the priest also!'

'The priest?' echoed Peter in surprise.

'Ay!' grinned Robin into his beard, 'or it will be the end of Robin Hood. Now do you understand right well the parts you must play?'

They nodded.

'I will not hide from you, lad,' he told Humphrey very gravely, 'that of all the tasks, yours is the most perilous. But all will go well if you be steadfast and lose not your wits. Now listen. When you have played your part, you must walk slowly away, and in the confusion—for confusion there will certainly be—you may well escape. Whatever betide, you must not run, nor show any sign of haste; for a crowd that is cheated is swift upon the scent as any hound. And if by ill chance you be taken, then submit yourself, for I will come to your aid, I pledge my word. Now, are you still willing?'

The boys nodded again, very earnestly.

'We are now seven furlongs from the city gates, and here we separate. We shall meet again by the oak-tree that stands three furlongs from the west gate of the city on the left-hand side. Now remember—the signal given, you must delay not an instant. It is a man's life you work for—and maybe your own and mine too! And so farewell and good luck go with us!'

Robin went striding down the road in his long black habit. Peter put his ship back into the pouch at his girdle and the three hastened towards the city.

Great crowds were still hurrying in through the gates towards the market-place, and it was only with difficulty that Peter managed to struggle towards the castle.

Humphrey found himself swept on with the crowd to the market-place. His heart was thudding so loudly that he thought the folk on either hand must stop to inquire what the strange noise could be. The market-place itself was black with people and he wondered how on earth he was to get anywhere near the stake.

Fortunately for him the crowd was in high humour and he pushed and nudged and edged nearer and nearer to the platform. There he stood, his face averted from the great pile of faggots, his eyes straining in the direction from which the procession must come.

Minute after minute went by. Then half an hour. An hour.

The hot sun beat down upon the boards of the scaffold, the pitch upon the faggots began to ooze and run.

'He'll need no fire to roast him!' chuckled a man who stood next to Humphrey. Humphrey laughed back and hated himself for laughing at the cruel jest.

'I reckon he be saying his prayers,' continued the man. 'To Old Nick, maybe!'

'He may well take his time about them,' grinned another, 'since they are the last he will ever say!'

'No chance for bold Robin to come to his help!' said the first man.

''Tis well so!' chuckled the second. 'Of all things I do like a good roasting!'

Humphrey said nothing. He went on smiling with his lips, but his heart was hot with anger against them. A man was to lose his life, an innocent man, and here they were, making merry and waiting to see the sight.

At last his heart leaped, so that for a moment he wondered whether he were going to be sick. In the distance he could see a dark group moving slowly.

And now the others had seen it too, and a shudder of excitement ran through the crowd. Men and women strained on tip-toe to miss nothing of the sight. Humphrey, his face chalk-white, stood perfectly still. Only his heart beat in his ears like the roaring of waves.

The procession moved slowly. First came the sheriff, and Humphrey knew him again by his great nose and his cold eyes. With him walked the Bishop of Lincoln, his gentle eyes cast to the ground. A little behind walked a fat and pursy churchman whom the crowd cheered, for the Prior of Lenton had been first to urge this day's treat. Then followed officers of the city, and soldiers on guard.

In the middle, still in torn and tattered green, walked the prisoner, with his hands bound behind him. He looked very young and very pale, but he carried his head high. He would not let the rabble know how he feared this horrible death, and one day Robin would avenge him. By his side walked a priest, his head bent in prayer.

Humphrey, his heart shaken with pity, watched them pass slowly by.

Now the procession had reached the platform, and the prisoner, stumbling a little, mounted the rough steps. As he stood there, blinking in the strong sunlight, fists were shaken in the air, and there arose from the crowd cries of anger.

The priest stepped close to the prisoner and spoke in a low voice, as if exhorting him to repent.

At this moment Humphrey rose to his feet, and as though he put back the hair from his eyes, raised the hand holding the cap. And while all eyes were fixed on the man who was to die he gave the signal three times in quick succession.

Suddenly a low murmur arose, so low that at first no man could catch the words. It grew louder and louder, and now all eyes were turned from the prisoner at the stake and stared upwards.

And good cause they had to stare.

For there, in the clear sky, like a great winged bat, hung a dark shape. Slowly it began to drop.

'The Devil! The Devil!' rose from pale lips, and panic-stricken, the crowd pushed in all directions, seeking wildly for safety.

The great winged shape descended, and with a swift movement, both prisoner and priest were caught up and carried aloft.

The crowd surged madly, fighting for safety. For a moment Humphrey stood still, rooted to the spot. All he had to do was walk quietly away. He knew that well enough. But he was frightened. He couldn't help it.

He broke into a run.

'Hey friend, wait for me!' bawled the man who had jested before. But Humphrey ran on.

And suddenly the man remembered. He had moved for a second to ease his weary limbs and from the corner of his eye he had seen the lad raise the cap above his head. He had not thought anything of it at the time, for his attention had been set upon the prisoner. But now all was clear.

'A witch!' he screamed. 'He brought the devil. I saw him make the spell!'

'A witch! A witch!' rang wildly to the sky.

'Burn him!'

'Ay, burn him in place of the one he saved!'

'See if he can save himself!'

'Burn! Burn!'

Humphrey ran on. He heard the cries and the fall of swiftly running feet. A stone whizzed behind his ear. He saw the west gate open and dashed blindly through.

He ran madly on. His breath was coming in quick gasps, but his heart was light. The man was saved.

He half-turned his head, and saw, hard upon his heels, the mad rush of the crowd. He tried to spur on his slackening feet. If he could reach the oak-tree! The others would be waiting, and he would be safe.

He was running more slowly now. His breath was coming in sobbing gasps that seemed to tear his chest in two.

Nearer and nearer drew the crowd.

'I'm done!' he thought desperately.

A hand reached to seize his shoulder and withdrew with a howl, an arrow sticking through the palm.

The dark bird swooped once more from the sky. Eager hands dragged him aboard.

Stones whizzed through the air and rattled harmlessly against the sides of the ship; but soon it had risen too high for any stone to reach, and was winging steadily towards Sherwood Forest.

'Phew!' sighed Robin, and threw off his priest's disguise.

The fresh keen air blew upon them, and soon the young man sat upright, looking about him as if he would never be weary of seeing the sun again. Now the boat began to descend, and soon they were standing knee-deep among the bracken. The young man stood looking about him, as though even now he could not believe he was alive and free.

'I had thought never to see the greenwood again,' he said. 'I thank you, Robin, with all my heart!'

'Nay Dickon, do not thank me,' said Robin gently. 'But give thanks to these children!'

Soon they came to a clearing in the forest where a great table was spread with venison and white bread, and wine both white and red, and apple pasties and honeycakes. Beneath a tall-spreading oak-tree Sheila sat talking to a fair lady clad in green, while Sandy listened, nibbling busily at a honeycake.

All three sprang to their feet as Robin and his party appeared, and loud and long and many were the explanations. They all laughed heartily when Robin explained how he had tricked the priest into finding food for the poor friar, and had locked him into his own cupboard after robbing him of his gown. And there, said Robin, he was likely to remain until his servant discovered him. 'But I will send him a piece of gold for the poor, to recompense him for my scurvy treatment!' he declared. 'And now, to our meat!'

The sun was slipping behind the tree-tops when Peter said they must go. All rose up in their places and drank a toast to the new-comers to the greenwood. Then Peter responded with thanks to gallant Robin who had trusted them with his life.

At last Peter drew the ship from his pouch and set it upon the ground. When it had grown large enough, the children stepped into it.

Suddenly Robin pushed Dickon forward. 'Take him with you,' he said. 'For here his life is no longer safe. They will comb the countryside until they take him again. Also, he has no great love for the greenwood, for his heart is set upon machines and such things as you have spoken about while we sat at meat. If he goes with you he will be both happy and safe.'

Peter looked at the others and they nodded.

The young man fell on his knees before Robin, then, rising, he raised Maid Marian's hand to his lips, and without once more looking backward, followed the others. His hand brushed the boar's head as he stepped aboard.

Dickon lay against the side of the boat. Now that the excitement of being free had worn off, he was overcome with exhaustion.

'You'll catch an awful cold!' said Peter, and put his own coat over Dickon's shoulders.

Soon they were through the dark cloud. The boat beached itself upon the wet sand. The children scrambled out and stood waiting for Dickon.

'Come on!' called Peter. There was no reply.

'Come *on*! he cried again, a little impatiently, for it was late and they were very tired.

No one answered.

Peter climbed back into the rapidly diminishing ship, but there was no one to be seen. It was quite, quite empty.

They searched anxiously, halloing at first softly, and then more and more loudly. But there was neither sight nor sound of Dickon. At last, wearily, they trailed homewards.

Slipping tiptoe into the sleeping house, they crept silently upstairs and into their warm and waiting beds.

Up in the playroom the children were discussing last night's adventure.

'What really did happen to that chap?' wondered Peter for the fiftieth time.

'Goodness knows!' declared Sheila. 'It *was* queer!'

'I expect he'll turn up somewhere or other!' said Sandy comfortably.

'I wonder what happened to my engine?' asked Humphrey thoughtfully. 'He had it in his hand when he got into the ship. I know because I saw it. He said the sheriff took it away from him during the trial, and then gave it back so that it could be burnt with him!'

'Horrible!' said Sheila, and she shuddered.

'Don't let's talk about it any more,' suggested Sandy, poking at the bottom of a sweet-bottle with a pencil to see if she could dislodge a bull's eye that had stuck in a corner.

'Got any swops?' asked Humphrey, obediently changing the subject. And soon his head and Peter's were bent over two stamp albums.

Sheila, who too was feeling tired after the night before, strolled lazily over to the bookcase, and taking her knitting from the drawer, began slowly to draw her needles through the wool.

'That chap *will* turn up again, I know he will!' said Peter suddenly.

'What makes you think so?' asked Humphrey.

'I don't know. But he'll turn up. You see if he doesn't!'

But day after day went by, and soon it was a whole week since the last adventure, and still there was no sign of Dickon.

It certainly did look as though the adventure was over and done with.

And then, one morning, something happened.

They were all sitting round the breakfast table in the dining-room, except father, who was standing by the window, *tutting* with vexation.

'The garden looks rotten,' he said disgustedly. 'Tiresome of Field to get himself another job, he was a good gardener. And that fellow of Robert's hasn't turned up. Well, I'm not going to wait for him any longer. He may be all Robert said, first-rate gardener, clever with the car and all that, but I cannot and will not wait for him a day longer!'

'He may turn up any minute, now,' said mother hopefully. 'Come along dear, your coffee's getting cold.'

Father strolled over to the table, and at this moment the side-door bell rang sharply.

The sound of the bell was quite clear in the dining-room, for Gertrude, who had just brought in some more toast, had left the door ajar. She put the toast-rack down and went out of the room, and across the hall and down the passage and through the kitchen where cook sat peacefully at the table blowing into her tea, and across the scullery.

Presently she returned. 'It's the new gardener, sir,' she said, 'and I've asked him to wait.'

That afternoon the four children went round to the potting-shed to make the acquaintance of the new gardener—after all, a lot of the fun you can have in the garden depends upon what sort of man the gardener is.

They found him bent over a box of seedlings, and hearing their footsteps, he turned round.

'Dickon!' said Humphrey under his breath.

'That's my name!' said the young man, 'though how you know it fair beats me. Dick Attwood at your service. And my friends always call me Dickon, same as you did! And now I come to think of it, I seem to know you too!' He gave them a long and puzzled look. 'But I can't think where. Have you ever been up at Pagham—that's Mr. Grey's place, Mr. Robert Grey?'

Peter shook his head.

'I could have sworn I'd seen you before,' Dick Attwood

went on. 'I expect I could place it, but I'm a bit muzzy still on account of an accident I had a week ago or thereabout. Nasty accident it was too. Knocked out by a chap on a motor-bike. At least that's what I think it was. He didn't stay long enough to let me make sure.'

'It's disgusting!' Sheila said indignantly. 'Knocking people down and not even stopping to see if they're hurt!'

'Might have knocked me out of my job, too!' Attwood said. 'And good jobs aren't too easy to come by. I was in luck your dad kept the place open for me!'

'We're jolly glad he did!' Humphrey told him warmly.

'We were wondering where you'd got to—' Sandy began. 'Ow—' for Sheila had suddenly and firmly stepped upon her toe.

'Nice of you I'm sure!' said Attwood. 'Seems like my luck's turned since I picked up my mascot. Look!'

His hand went to his pocket, and the children stared at the object upon his outstretched palm.

Humphrey picked up his engine with fingers that trembled a little. 'Wherever did you find it?' he asked.

'Picked it up! I walked over from Radcliff this morning. I was taking a short cut across the beach that some one told me of. And there it was, sticking up as perky as you please! Nice little thing, isn't it?'

'It's Humphrey's!' cried Sandy, dancing about on one foot. 'The one he lost ages and ages ago!'

Attwood looked at the toy regretfully. 'Now I've got to. part with my mascot just when it made my luck turn!'

Humphrey pressed the engine back into Attwood's hand.

235

'Keep it,' he said. 'I'd like you to. Awfully. And I hope it brings you luck!'

And so it did! At least, that's what Attwood always said.

CHAPTER 16
The Flying-ship Goes Home

Time was slipping away. The children were growing up little by little, even Sandy was getting quite big. And it was five years since Peter had seen the magic ship in an old dark window.

And very good use they made of it, too. Backwards and forwards through History they went, until the story of their country became a living glowing world to them.

They saw the island of Runnymede abloom with summer—and John, fierce yet helpless, ringed about with those barons who forced him to sign the charter of English liberty. They saw Cœur-de-Lion, handsome and ruddy and cruel; and that other gentle Richard who lost his crown and his life. They rode in procession from The Tabard Inn, and listened to those enchanting tales that fell from the lips of Master Chaucer. They saw Elizabeth with her painted face and her orange curls, and her strange wise eyes, and they trembled in their shoes before her royal fury. And once they saw Mary Stuart and looked with wonder and pity into her fair sad face. They saw Charles and covered their eyes with their hands when he went proudly to his death through the early morning mist.

And they went farther and farther back in time, until often

it seemed that the time-cloud would never lift. They walked in the hanging gardens of Babylon, they watched beside Leonidas in the pass of Thermopylae, they stood with Horatius when he kept the bridge, and stepped beside Hannibal over the frozen Alps when he marched for Rome.

And when they were weary of the glories of the past, then the boat took them swiftly through the air to the vast steppes of Russia and the strange Indian lands. They saw the sacred haunts of the Dalai Lama, and the gorgeous African forests where the Pygmy people live.

It was all so wonderful and so magical that sometimes they got a little confused in their adventures, so that their memories were like a painted pattern that some one has left out in the rain. And sometimes they began to wonder whether it was really true—all of them except Peter, who had no doubts whatever.

And as the days went by, they began to believe more and more that these adventures had never really happened, but that they were wonderful tales that Peter told. The story of Usertsen was a good one, they thought, but of course they had never actually talked to the boy who sat with the royal crown of Egypt upon his head and his hand upon a yellow lion. And they liked the tale of Robin and Dickon and the greenwood, but it had never really happened, for wouldn't Dick have remembered? Certainly Dick could not have forgotten!

No, Peter could tell the most marvellous stories, he was going to be an author when he grew up—and they were always ready to listen. But pretend that they really *believed*—well, that was just too silly!

Only Peter went on believing all by himself. Sometimes he would take the magic ship out of his pocket, and stroke it gently as if it were something alive that had been unkindly treated; then he would put it back again into his pocket. He did not care to take it on an adventure any more since the others would not come. Or, if on a rare occasion he could persuade them, they would talk about it afterwards as one of Peter's tales.

No, the fun had gone out of it.

And then Peter began to wonder what would happen if he, too, grew like the others and didn't believe. His boat, his own little boat, would be neglected and forgotten. And the magic would work no longer—for when you no longer believe, then the magic stops.

And then he remembered after all these years a promise he had made when he had first had the boat—a promise that one day he would send it back. And if like the others, he should come to believe in the boat no longer, why then that promise could never be kept.

Suddenly Peter knew what he must do. He must return the boat before he grew like the others. He must find the little dark shop and give back the flying-boat before it was too late. Once more he took the little boat up in his hands and looked at it long and lovingly. He stroked the tiny gilt head of the boar with the tip of his finger. To-night he would return the ship!

But why to-night? Why couldn't he keep it a day or two longer? Just one day? Because if he kept it only a day longer, he would never bring himself to part with it, never. And it must be at night, when every one was asleep, or the others would ask where he was going and they would offer to go with him; and since they no longer believed, he would never find the shop again.

It was quite dark when Peter slipped out of bed. The moonlight lay in patches of silver upon the floor. The curtains moved gently in the breeze. It was all so exactly like that first night of adventure when they had gone to see mother in the nursing-home, that he longed to awaken the others and take them on one last adventure. He wanted tremendously to prove to them that his ship was really and truly magic.

Humphrey turned over in bed and threw out an arm. In a panic lest Humphrey should wake up and discover what he was going to do, Peter crouched down in bed again. For several minutes he lay perfectly still listening to the sound of Humphrey's soft and even breathing, then, very cautiously he crept once more out of bed. Hardly daring to breathe, he sat down on the floor in the moonlight and put on his clothes. Then, his shoes in his hand, his bare feet making no sound on the polished boards, he crept over to the window and put the flying-ship down on the sill.

'Take me back to the shop where I first saw you,' he whispered. The ship began to grow.

When it was large enough to hold just one, Peter stepped inside. He could not help feeling sad when he remembered how the boat used to grow until it was big enough to hold four, and how they had all scrambled on board, their hearts beating high at the thought of adventure.

The Flying-ship Goes Home

And now he was to make this last adventure alone.

Up went the ship through the dark night sky. His arm thrown about the neck of the golden boar, Peter thought, 'The last time. The very last!'

The boat sank and settled very gently. Peter stepped along the deserted promenade holding the boat tightly in his hand. He passed the empty pierrot shack on the beach, and made his way towards the dark and empty bandstand. Suddenly he looked up. At his right hand a dark and crooked street stretched away before him. The moonlight fell upon overhanging roofs and white plaster and black old beams. His heart beating fit to choke him, Peter strode up the narrow crooked street.

There it was! The old, old shop with the bay window lit up in the moonlight so that everything was as clear as day. There was the old oak table, and the blue-and-white saucers and the string of dusty beads. He found himself wondering whether they were magic beads—and what would happen if you bought them. The eyes of bottle-glass in the window-pane winked slyly.

Nothing was changed. Nothing at all. Except that there was a clear space on the dusty old table where a little ship had once stood.

Peter put his hand to the door. It opened easily at his touch. 'Almost as if some one was expecting me,' he thought, a little frightened. A faint tinkle sounded at the back of the shop. He stood alone in the moonlight among objects that might be precious beyond any counting, or mere junk that nobody wanted at all. He dared not move in case he swept something off with his elbow, or trod on something with his foot.

He stood there holding the little boat in his hand, and wanting more than anything in the world to run right away with it, when he heard a movement at the back of the shop. There was first of all a little rustle, then a dry little cough, and then the soft clop-clop of slippers.

And then, quite suddenly, the old man stood before him, a black patch over one eye, and smiling kindly at him.

Without a word Peter held out the boat.

Without a word the old man took it, and turned it about. For a long time he stood in silence, examining it closely, then at last he spoke. 'You have used it much,' he said, 'and you. have used it well. These scratches now,' and he pointed to the marks that the flying stones had scored when they had saved Dickon from the mob. 'These scratches have saved a man's life!' and he nodded at Peter.

Peter stared. How on earth did the old fellow know that?

The old man nodded again. 'I know everything,' he said. 'Everything!'

Peter went on staring. He had seen this old man before, only then he had been dressed differently. Peter couldn't remember very clearly, but it might have been like a king. Or had he perhaps a helmet of gold upon his head—a winged helmet? Or was it maybe, a broad hat to shade him from the sun? He racked his brains trying to remember. But it was useless.

'You have forgotten,' said the old man. 'And you will forget still more!'

'I don't want to forget,' cried Peter, 'I don't want to!'

The old man leaned over and touched Peter's forehead with his finger. It was a pleasant touch, cool and soothing.

'Of course you must forget,' he said kindly. 'You must make room for all the new things you have to learn.'

'I don't understand,' said Peter.

'A chest will hold so much and no more!' said the old man. 'If you put new things in, why then you must take old things out! It is very simple!'

He opened the drawer beneath the counter and took out two silver shillings, a sixpence, a threepenny bit, and three pennies. He held them out to Peter so that the moonlight fell full upon them.

Peter put his hands behind his back. He could not bear the thought of selling his beloved ship. He preferred to give it back, a free gift.

Again the old man shook his head.

'It remains yours until you take back the purchase price. And if you will not take back the purchase price,' he said very softly, 'why then, the ship will never return to Frey.'

In silence Peter held out his hand and took the money.

'Once,' said the old man still very softly, 'a promise was made to you. Have you forgotten? Listen, I will repeat it. *When you shall return the flying-ship to its rightful owner, then I will give you in return your heart's desire!*'

'I know you,' Peter cried out suddenly, 'I *know* you! You are—you are—'

He shivered as the night wind blew about him, for he stood alone on the empty promenade.

There was a faint hint of light in the sky, and Peter dropped over the railings on to the sand. The tide was going out and the sand was firm underfoot. He sat down on a boulder of white chalk and took off his shoes. He fastened the laces together and slung them round his neck. Then he set out.

As he walked along he remembered that other time he had sauntered homeward across the beach, the magic ship in his pocket. Well that had been the beginning of the adventure, and this was the end.

He began to run over the firm ribbed sand, for it was chilly before the coming of dawn. A faint rosy streak showed in the sky, and then another, and another. The sky was streaked with light, the sea lay warm with rosy light.

Something was heavy in his hand. Oh yes, the money that the old man had given him. He stopped and looked at it.

This money, he thought, was quite different from any other money in the whole world, since it had twice bought and sold the magic ship. And now it should never buy or sell anything again.

He ran lightly to the water's edge. His arm went up high above his head. With a swift gesture he cast the coins out over the water. The sun caught them as they fell, and turning sharply, he could have sworn to a chuckle at his elbow—a chuckle as though some one were pleased with him.

And suddenly, it was as if casting away the money, he had cast away his unhappiness. The sun was up and the morning was fine. He stepped along briskly, whistling as he went. There was a warmth in the air as he crept up the garden path, through the dining-room window which some one had carelessly left unlatched, and up the silent stairs to bed.

Whether all this really happened, not even Peter can say now.

He had awakened after what had been an unusually vivid dream to find the ship gone. And it was then, looking down at his empty hand, that he began to wonder whether the others were right. Perhaps there had never been a magic ship after all, perhaps nobody had ever promised them a gift in exchange.

Maybe. Maybe not. But whether the old man really gave them a gift or whether he didn't, all of them were happy and successful for the rest of their lives.

Peter became a writer. The people who understand these things said that he was a very good writer indeed. Everybody wanted to read Peter's books, and so he sold thousands and thousands and thousands. And if that isn't lucky, I don't know what is!

Sheila became a doctor. She was a very good doctor—clever and patient and kind. She went on writing poetry, and people who knew about poetry said she was a real poet.

Humphrey became an archaeologist—as he always wanted to. One evening he went out to dinner—it was a special archaeologists' dinner, and found himself sitting next to John Nickalls. It was a queer meeting, because although they were strangers to each other and had to tell each other their names, each was sure they had met before. But neither could think where. But soon they were chatting away like old friends, and when Nickalls asked Humphrey whether he would like to join forces, Humphrey said he would. Nickalls was still working on the inscriptions in the rock tomb of Usertsen near Thebes. There was, he said, enough work to last your whole life long. And so there was!

And as for Sandy, she got married and had a lot of children—as she always said she would. And she scolded them and loved them—as she always said she would. And when Uncle Peter came to tea, and Sandy's children begged him for a story, he always told them of the adventures of a flying-ship that four lucky children found.

And every one who knew Peter and Sheila and Humphrey and Sandy when they were grown-up, called them The Lucky Grants.

So there does seem to be something in it after all.